PROMISES
TO
KEEP

by

Marcella DiPaolo

For copyright permission requests, or for information about special discounts available for bulk purchases, sales promotions, or educational needs, write to or e-mail the publisher at one of the following addresses.

Phantasy Publishing LLC
35 Brooks Drive
Bethalto, IL 62010

Website: www.phantasypublishing.com
E-mail: support@phantasypublishing.com

This is a work of fiction. Names, characters, places, and incidents are either the products of the author's imagination, or they are used fictitiously. Any resemblance to actual persons, living or dead, businesses, companies, events, or locales is entirely coincidental.

Published in the United States of America

Table of Contents

CHAPTER 1

The Ozarks in the State of Missouri (Present Day)

'Oh, Kate ... ' the letter read, 'I need your help... 'The forehead of the young girl creased in thought. With a sigh she put the letter down. A shadow crossed the delicate lines of her face. Her hand pushed the heavy strands of hair from her eyes. She crossed to the window of the sun-drenched room. Her hair seemed to catch fire as the gentle rays of mornings first light touched the russet tendrils of Kate's silken cap. Crossing her arms in front of her, she leaned heavily against the small panes of the windowed wall.

The view was breathtaking. Sunrise in the Ozark hills of Missouri. Dew sparkled like diamonds on the uncut grass and virgin timber. There was the endless babbling of the nearby brook. The songs of a dozen birds filled the air. At the edge of the clearing, deer scampered, knowing they were safe from hunters. Squirrels played beneath the leafy foliage.

Without thought, Kate reached for her camera, adjusting her settings deftly, quickly reloading for another roll, time seemed suspended. Several hours and many rolls later, Kate rolled up her sleeves and ran a tired hand through her hair. She raised her arms slowly and rolled head to ease fatigued muscles. Her shadow was thrown against the wall. Even in well-worn Levi's and a faded flannel shirt, there was no mistaking Kate's diminutive but shapely curves. Silently crossing the wooden floor to the transmitter radio,

Kate turned on the generator, the motor an alien sound in the stark almost bare cabin.

"Red-O to Big D... Come in please." she paused, checking her watch; she smiled at the knowledge that Max would probably still be sleeping.

"Red-O to Big-D...Wake up sleepyhead!" Kate said into the small speaker again. A muffled sound came from the box. Kate grinned flicking the transmitter switch. "I heard you grown Max, Good morning to you, too!" she chuckled, "Go get a cup of coffee. Stella always leaves it ready for you. I'll wait." She paused, again picking up the letter, tapping it against the table.

Minutes later, a deep voice broke the silence, "Big-D here ... I think... what's up Red?"

"I just finished the pictures; I'll develop them this afternoon. That should finish the series up, Max" she waited.

"Great! Way to go, Red, when do I see the proofs?"

"I'll drive up tomorrow morning. It'll take a while to pack up the equipment and everything." Again, she paused, "Is there anything coming up that can't wait a while Max?"

Silence filled the room, "What's wrong, Red? You never ask for time off."

"Then it's about time I did," Kate responded, "All work and no play makes me a dull girl."

"I'll agree to a vacation for you Kate, but as to you, you are never being dull, never!!!" he paused, "but something is wrong, Give, Red ... Why the sudden urge to play?"

"I'll explain tomorrow." Kate answered, "I'll be in by noon. Do you think Stella would mind if she had an extra mouth to feed?"

"Not if it's yours! Alright Kate, I'll wait till tomorrow for explanations. I'll start work on an extended vacation, OK?"

"OK...and thanks, Max. Ten, four, over and out." Kate responded, flicking the button. Her eyes traveled around the room,

2

mentally searching for those items she needed to begin the developing of the film. Picking up her camera and the timer she headed for the back door closing it silently behind her. The room was dimly lit and shadowed, showing only tables and pans. Kate began the process of transforming her negatives into actual proofs. It was past three o'clock when she finished, smiling to herself at the photos of the squirrels playing amongst the leaves.

Not bad, Kate thought, this ought to satisfy her client and Max. She opened the door letting in fresh air and the afternoons light. Kate grabbed a towel from the small table and lit the kerosene lamp on the table, knowing the evening's shadows would already be present when she returned home. Outside she reached for her pole and without breaking stride crossed the clearing to the bubbling stream. She tossed out her line, settling against the tree trunk nearest the bank. Kate waited patiently for the familiar pull of the string. Her wait was rewarded as the line grew tight. Kate let out the line, letting the fish tire itself out. Slowly Kate began to run the reel, the flicker of a tail splashing the water rushing past. Seconds later, a rainbow trout lay beside Kate on the grass. Kate washed in the creek and then gathered up her pole and catch, headed back to the cabin.

She stocked up the fireplace, and placed her fish and a potato, both wrapped in foil on the grate covering the embers. While they cooked Kate made coffee and sliced a tomato. She took the last of the sour dough bread and buttered and toasted it above the flames.

Taking her dinner off the grill, Kate replaced it by a kettle of water, enough for washing her few dishes and a more thorough wash for herself. Kate took her time, the lengthening shadows upon the wall, the chirping of frogs and crickets began to fill the silence. Her unhurried movements were graceful, unwasted, as those of much practice. Finishing, she began to pack her few belongings into an old green Army duffle bag. Within minutes the cabin had lost what few luxuries it contained, and the precious proofs and cameras had been carefully packed away.

She stretched, yawned and turned her lamp off throwing the room into darkness. Moonlight beamed through the window; a star flecked sky its background. Kate lay down, pulling her sleeping bag firmly around her shoulders. Sleep came within minutes, her last thoughts of the letter she held in her hand.

She rose quickly, just as dawn filtered through the window. Rolling her sleeping bag, she tied it to her backpack. Slipping her arms through the straps, she picked up her duffel bag in one hand, her camera case in the other she walked out the door. Carefully closing and latching the heavy wooden door. She followed a trail that was almost hidden from sight. Her steps quiet, soundless, despite her heavy load. Two miles through the woods, Kate stopped, shifted her backpack and continued a few hundred feet farther. A dilapidated barn stood in the clearing, its doors hanging by rusty hinges. Kate pushed the door, disturbing the dust as she opened It. Stowing her gear in the jeep, she was relieved that the weight had been removed from her shoulders. She was soon on the narrow road leading into town.

Several hours later, Kate drove up to a huge home in Branson, Missouri. The doorbell of the stately Colonial home rang, echoing dully down the thick carpeted halls. As Kate was shown in, she heard Stella's voice singing slightly off key as usual. Kate smiled, "I'll find her myself" she informed the butler and following the notes of 'Somewhere over the Rainbow' Kate emerged into Stella's kitchen just in time to join her for the chorus.

Kate was engulfed in a hug by the slightly plump, grey haired woman, her apron askew, her eyes sparkling, immediately disapproving, over Kate's faded jeans and shirt.

"You're too early for lunch but just in time to change into something 'nice' before lunch, young lady," clicking her

4

disapproval. "I can't understand you girl, with a figure such as yours and covering it up with such gruesome clothes and losing yourself in the backs of beyond! How do you ever plan on getting your man, looking like that, and hiding yourself away?!"

Kate laughed at the familiar voice, "My man will look beyond clothes to see me, love that is if he exists. Maybe, I was just cut out to be an old spinster."

"Humph!" Stella snorted. "Over my dead body! Now off with you and make yourself presentable or I'll not be feeding you any of my chocolate cake."

"Oh, Stella," Kate grinned, "you've said the magic word. I give up and I'll change, at least for dinner." She smiled," Maybe the way to a man's heart is through his stomach. Does it work Stella?"

Stella's pink cheeks betrayed her, and Kate ducked as she tossed the dishtowel at her as she fled out the kitchen door. Thirty minutes later, one would never recognize Kate for the same girl who appeared at lunch. Her hair freshly washed, shining, vibrantly alive. She was dressed in an old-fashioned frilly cream-colored blouse with a high collar and large puffed sleeves. Small narrow pleats trimmed with lace decorated the bodice, and the full peasant skirt made Kate appear as feminine as the Victorian lady who had first pioneered her dress.

Max was already seated; he lifted his gnarled cheek for Kate's welcoming kiss.

"It's always good to have you back," he began gruffly, "in one piece. Why anyone that looks like you should go gallivanting off to take pictures of animals is beyond me!"

"I suppose that's a compliment, "Kate grinned, "Thanks, love, but to put your mind at rest, you know I'm perfectly capable of handling myself all alone in the woods and besides taking pictures is what I do best. So ...?"

"So?" he returned, a dull flush appearing in his cheeks making even more of a contrast to his white hair. "You should be meeting young men, having babies, getting married, and don't be so sassy, not in that order!"

Helping herself to a serving of salad, Kate retorted, "You're right Max, and I'll make a deal with you. As soon as you make an honest woman of Stella," (at which Max almost choked) "I'll find myself a fella and settle down. I believe the old adage is 'Monkey see, monkey do?"

"That's not what I had in mind," he began gruffly.

"I know dear, "Kate said contritely," but here I am only twenty-six, and well you're not getting any younger. How long has Stella been around spoiling you?"

"Katherine O'Hara," Max said firmly, "Stella's relationship with me is none of your concern!"

"Uh-Uh, your happiness is my concern. You worry about me. Why can't I worry about you? You need a wife." Kate sat back and studied her friend. Poor Max she thought as he blustered and sat dumbfounded at Kate's words. She smiled, "I love you Max and I know Stella does, too. Why else would she have put up with you for all these years?" She paused, letting Max digest her words, "I know that you love Stella, Max. There's no law or rule that says you can't fall in love and get married after you're sixty years old." She put her napkin down and stood up. She laid her hand on Max's arm, "Forgive my interference, old friend, I'm an incurable romantic, I'd like to see everyone as happy as Da and Ma were. I... I just don't want anyone to wait till it's too late. The time we spend with someone we love is never time enough."

As she bent to brush her lips against Max's head, he forestalled her exit by covering her hand by his own. Max cleared his throat, as he squeezed her hand, "Now about that time off ..."

Kate sat back down and sighed, "Its Patrick, Max. Leigh's having a bit of trouble with her pregnancy. I'd like to go and give him a little moral support. I'll be back as soon as baby Ryan makes a healthy entrance. I promise!" She laughed, "And just think of the pictures I'll get of my niece or nephew!"

"Mama Ryan to the rescue, huh?" Max teased. "Keep the picture idea though, I'm working on an exhibit of your pictures, they'd be a good addition."

"It's all clear then?"

"Just as soon as I can see your last proofs of the wildlife series. Are they as good as the others?"

Kate grinned and spoke modestly, "I like them, Max. Wait till you see them!" She pulled the portfolio off the desk and began spreading out the pictures.

Max looked at the pictures carefully, studying the detail and clarity of each one. His sparkling eyes betrayed his pleasure and delight in Kate's performance. "Well, what do you think?" Kate asked anxiously, unconsciously biting her lower lip.

"How do you do it, Kate? How do you take a picture that talks without words? Look at these...these animals seem almost human!"

Kate laughed a golden husky sound, "When you live with them, they seem human. Each one has a different personality, some are shy, others very aggressive, they show jealousy, and possessiveness. But most of all they show love and joy at just doing simple things." She sighed, "I'll never get tired of watching animals and children."

"You need a few of your own," Max added wryly.

"But first I need to get married, right?! Which takes us full circle, I spend so much time in the woods how will I ever meet someone, to fall in love, etcetera ... I'll tell you what, I'll look around when I'm at Pat's and with any luck... who knows," she grinned wickedly, "I could trade in my camera for a wedding ring."

Stella chose that moment to enter bearing her chocolate cake--
"Ah, Stella," began Kate, "Max and I were just talking about you..."

St. Louis, Missouri (Present Day)

"Damnit, Morgan! What are we going to do now?" demanded the tall, slim man as he walked briskly through the door, not bothering to knock. "We have a deadline to meet and somewhere, somehow we have to find a secretary who's trustworthy, efficient and will stay for a lot longer than the last few have. You do realize you've gone through four in the last two months?" he went on to add sarcastically, pushing a hand through his blond hair. He looked across the room at the dark figure sitting at the desk.

Morgan Buchanan watched his friend and partner, wondering for the umpteenth time how two such opposites could be so close. His friend Patrick Ryan was the All American blue-eyed blond boy from next door. He was the son of Irish American parents, a close-knit family from the tales he told. Warm, outgoing, people trusted Patrick Ryan on sight, and with good reason, he was a man of his word. Morgan thought back to the first time he had met Patrick at college.

Pat was there on a scholarship and a shoestring budget. They had been assigned as roommates. Four years of watching him work part time jobs and studying till the wee hours of the morning to make up for lost time earned Morgan's respect. Though from different backgrounds a strong bond was merged, a bond strong enough that eight years later they had formed their own company, R&B Computers, Inc. Morgan designed them, and Patrick built them. Morgan Buchanan was the most sought-after bachelor in St. Louis. His family was very wealthy, but he had chosen to make his own fortune. His jet-black hair and dark flashing eyes belied his Latin blood. Strong powerful shoulders flexed beneath the expensive blue shirt he wore. Muscular legs stretched to rest on the corner of his massive oak desk. He gave a cynical smile to the man across the room.

"Maybe we should hire a Boy Scout? I hear they're trustworthy, loyal and courageous enough to work at least long enough to break our last secretary's record."

"Which was three days?" Patrick said quietly. "Either they swoon at your feet or you chase them away with that temper of yours." He sighed, "Just for the record Morgan, what was the finale about?"

"She screwed up the files, I couldn't find the one I needed, when I asked her about it, she started crying and left."

"Asked? Or demanded?"

"I can't stand incompetence, Pat! She was terrified of my every word. If it hadn't been today, it would have been tomorrow!" He sighed, raising one eyebrow, "You wouldn't reconsider having Leigh come, back would you?"

"No." Pat said firmly. "If I didn't think it would hurt her or the baby, I wouldn't mind her working back in the office, but I won't let her take a chance. She's doing fine now but these last few months have been so difficult for her. I'm selfish. I want her to take it easy until that baby arrives safely." He smiled to ease the seriousness of his words, "I guess it's my entire fault that I married the only secretary that you could work with!"

"The problem wasn't that you married her, it wasn't until she became pregnant that we ran into trouble." He smiled, "I want to become a godfather almost as much as you want to be a father, Pat, I shouldn't have even mentioned Leigh, I'm sorry..."

The shrill ringing of the telephone interrupted him, picking up the phone he responded, "Buchanan ... Yes, he's here ... Just a minute ... Patrick, it's for you." Handing the phone to his friend, he went to stand by the window of his office.

"Leigh? Are you all right...What? ... You're kidding! That's great! For how long? ... Let me talk to her... Kate? ... It's great to hear from you! You'll stay with us, of course ... How did everything go? Okay, I'll see you tonight... Leigh? Everything all taken care of... I love you, too. See you tonight!"

Bright blue eyes met the dark brown ones of Morgan, "Don't tell me," he said, "you need to get home to meet another of your infamous relatives, right?!"

"Right! After all it's not as if we can get any work done, what without a secretary and all," he quipped, "I'll call the agency in the morning, this time we'll be lucky!"

"Your optimism depresses me," Morgan replied, "Go home, we'll settle things in the morning. Give my love to Leigh."

"Night, Morgan!" Patrick said, whistling as he went back through the door, his mind already on his wife and visitor.

Morgan sat at his desk, his eyes following his friend's exit, an almost envious expression crossing his face. Slowly he picked up the phone, dialing a number, he listened for the ring. "Brooke...Morgan here. How about dinner... Good ... I'll pick you up in an hour ..." He chuckled at the husky voice over the phone, "Save it ... we'll eat at your place, and then ... see you soon." He smiled, wryly, it might not be such a bad day after all, and he followed in Patrick's wake and left.

CHAPTER 2

Patrick whistled as he drove his car through the congested St. Louis streets. Kate, it sure would be good to see her! A smile broke out on his face, little Katie, how she used to hate that title. His mind wondered back to the first time he had met Kate so many years ago.

It had been early summer; the trees were a lush deep green in the Ozark hills of Missouri. It was their first vacation; he had been twelve at the time, his brothers Sean, Michael, and Danny stair steps behind him. They had rented a cabin for the summer. His father was a writer and felt the fresh country air would do his sons good after living all their lives in the city. Besides which, he could write anywhere. The first week was a nightmare! No television, or electricity had taken a little getting used to--not to mention the scary sounds from the woods surrounding them.

They had finally convinced their mother to let them swim or rather paddle in the creek by the house. They had splashed happily for a few minutes when stepping back Danny went under. The creek bed dropped suddenly and the undercurrents that carried so many canoes down the Ozark Rivers quickly did the same to Danny. Sean ran for help while Mike and Pat ran beside the bank. There was a tree branch over hanging the creek and sitting on the limb was a small figure capped with a red ponytail. Seeing Dan in the water, she swung down and caught his shirt, and helped him climb onto the limb. Mike and Pat reached Danny seconds later, relief flooded their faces as they saw Danny was safe, a short-lived relief as the redhead turned on the boys, emerald eyes flashing, and "Don't any of you guys swim? What a dumb thing to do! Don't you know your brother could have drowned?"

Numbly the boys had shaken their heads, surprise at the attack making them silent. In the distance they could hear their mother calling, "Pat! Mike! Where's Danny?" His father and mother arrived breathless with Sean. They gathered Danny in their arms.

"It's your fault." A tiny voice spoke up, defiantly, "What kind of parents are you? Why were you letting your kids in the creek when they can't even swim?"

The astonished eyes of his parents turned toward the tiny little girl. "She saved Danny," Patrick had volunteered.

"I'm not a she, the name is Katherine O'Hara, and they call me Kate." She pulled herself up straight to a full three feet plus inches, her head held high, her chin lifted.

"Thank you for your help, Miss O'Hara...er ... Kate, we appreciate it more than we can say," John Ryan began, "If you would take us to your parents, I'd like to tell them about the heroic action of their daughter."

"Can't." Kate replied flatly.

"Why not, Kate? I'm sure they'd be very proud of you," Anna Ryan said, her blond hair falling softly around her shoulders.

"I don't have any parents, they left me at the home when I was a baby, they weren't very proud of me then, I doubt this would make a difference." Her words were so adult yet spoken with a defiance that would tolerate no pity.

"Where do you live, Kate," John asked respecting the feisty little girl for her dignity.

"Other side of the hill," Kate replied. "I go where I want long as I'm back for meals and lights out. The sisters can't keep track of us all and besides, "she grinned, a small dimple appearing in her cheek, "Father Hannigan loves to eat the fish I catch." She told them nonchalantly. "I'll teach you if you like."

And so, it began. Kate seemed to know everything about the creek and the woods. Unofficially she was adopted by the Ryan's, John and Anna included. She became the daughter they didn't have, the little sister the boys adored. She bossed them all summer, teaching them where to fish and how to swim, where to find the sweetest mushrooms, and the deer at play. Which snakes to avoid and which they could catch. From city boys, they became adept country lads.

At summer's end, John and Anna could not bear the thought of leaving Kate. They filed for adoption. They were refused. Although they had enough money for their needs, with four growing boys, the courts thought one more would be one too many. Kate watched them go from the top of the hill, her russet hair shining, the wind blowing tendrils across her face. Tears blurred her vision of the only family she had ever known. The Ryan's were broken hearted; they vowed to return to the Ozark hills and their little Katie.

Through the long fall and winter letters passed. A Christmas box was sent by the Ryan's, and one received, Kate had finally sat still long enough to knit potholders for Anna, and socks for the boys and John. Anna cried fresh tears for the absence of her Katie.

Spring arrived and with it the plans for returning to the cabin. Kate was waiting for them. The cabin freshly swept and dusted, 'lilies of the valley' proudly decorating the center of the table. Kate was crushed to them.

Each year followed as the last, there were new things to learn and do. Each year they were again refused adoption. The boys grew into young men and Kate became a lively young lady. On her eighteenth birthday, she was officially released from the orphanage; she went to live with the Ryan's. Mike and Danny were finishing up at college, Sean was serving in the navy, and Patrick was working in a computer company in Texas, they all came to welcome her with open arms. Katie had finally come home.

Kate took a secretarial course and got a job with a small company. She brought fresh life into the Ryan house, life, joy, laughter and love. Two years later, John, Da discovered he had cancer. It was Kate who quit her job, and worked each day with Da, finishing his articles, taking the occasional picture to accompany them, helping Anna care for him. Kate kept their hopes alive. Three years later, Da died quietly in his sleep, his beloved family gathered around him ... his wife, his four sons, and his daughter. Anna lived for less than a year without her precious husband beside her. The doctors said she had heart failure, but Kate knew that she really died from a broken heart.

Patrick walked into his living room, smiling as he saw his light brown-haired wife laughing at Kate. Kate's emerald eyes were dancing as she watched Patrick cross the room to kiss first his wife and then her.

"Spare the ribs, Pat! Please!" Kate laughed.

"Well, if you'd ever grow to a decent size," he responded.

"Haven't you ever heard good things come in little packages?" Kate quipped, "I thought sure that's what Leigh was talking about! Aren't I the little visitor you were expecting?"

"For the first time Kate, you're too big!" Pat laughed, tucking an arm around Leigh, "Our little visitor will be even smaller than you!"

"He or she?!" Kate replied, "Not a big bruiser like my brothers! Wouldn't a nice tiny little girl with Leigh's eyes be much easier to handle?"

"He or she, WE don't care, as long as it's healthy and Leigh's all right," Patrick declared firmly, his eyes resting lovingly on his wife.

"Come on you two," Leigh said kissing his chin, "Let's eat, I'm sure you're starved!"

Over a delicious roast, Leigh, Pat and Kate talked. Kate's lively wit had tears rolling down Leigh's cheeks as she listened to their exchanging banter.

"Stop, please!" Leigh cried laughing, "Talk about something serious, my sides can't take much more!"

Patrick was instantly serious, his hand reaching to squeeze hers, "Are you alright, love?" He helped her up and carefully sat her on the sofa.

"I'm fine, in fact I've never felt better, and Kate's the best medicine I've taken in a long time. I just need a rest from laughing so much!"

"Sorry," Kate said, at once serious, "I know you've had a rough couple of months. Actually, that's one of the reasons I came. Could I be of any service helping? Cooking, cleaning, whatever! I'm at your service!"

"So that's why you came!" Pat grinned, "I wondered at the sudden visit ... Not that we don't feel honored, of course."

"Of course!" Kate returned cheekily. Then grew serious. "I can take it easy for a while, I'm not destitute you know, besides I'm between assignments and might as well be useful." She paused.

Pat looked across at Leigh, her answering smile as she knew his thoughts. "You're more than welcome to stay here sis, for as long as possible, as long as you can put up with us in fact," he assured her.

"No housework though," Leigh added. "I've become a woman of leisure. Pat's hired a maid and cook to come in regularly. I really do little enough around here except get bigger! I'd love the company!"

"So long as I'm useful," Kate laughed, "I've never been very good at sitting still doing nothing!"

Patrick sat up straight. His joking manner disappearing, "Kate, are you serious about being useful and staying around here for a while?"

"Why...yes... I am...What's wrong?"

"How about going to work for me?"

"What?!" Kate and Leigh asked simultaneously.

"We lost our fourth secretary today. We're on a crucial timetable. Our plans and designs have to be on the manufacturer's desk in six weeks or we lose the contract. We can't just take anybody; it's got to be someone we can trust. Kate, you're perfect!" Patrick stated triumphantly.

"Pat, why have you gone through four secretaries?" Kate asked suspiciously.

"Is Morgan, up to his usual sweet disposition?" Leigh inquired.

"The last one was scared of him; it wasn't his fault!" Pat defended him.

"And the other three, "Leigh added with a smile, "fell for him, right?"

"Right," Pat agreed hesitantly. "But... Kate is different. We know she's efficient, and we know she won't be cowed under by Morgan's ... er ... personality, and I don't think you'll fall for him. Will you?" he asked.

"Will I what?" Kate questioned softly, "Will I fall for him? Will I be cowed by him? Or will I even accept the job?"

Patrick looked at her perplexed, for once his tongue at a loss for words.

Leigh smiled, "He's not as bad as it sounds, Kate. I used to work for him. He's demanding, yes, but you've held a demanding job for the past three years, that won't be a problem. He is one of the richest, most eligible bachelors in St. Louis, not to mention very good looking! Women fall at his feet. Do you see that as a problem?"

"I can't imagine falling at any man's feet!" Kate declared, "Can you?!"

"NO!" This time Leigh and Patrick responded in unison. "You're perfect, Kate," Pat spoke firmly. "We'd sure appreciate it. You'd be helping us out of a tough spot. I want this project finished as soon as possible so that when the stork arrives; I can devote all my time to Leigh and the baby for a while." He paused, "Will you do it?"

"Sure," Kate grinned; "I'd have agreed five minutes ago, but I love to see you squirm, Pat!" she ducked as a pillow landed beside her head.

Leigh laughed, "Tell us more about your job, Kate. Patrick needs a break; he's not used to being given such a rough time!"

Kate grinned, tossing back the pillow, "Sure, but there's not much to tell, I freelance pictures and articles very similar to Da's only because of my interest in nature, I guess I lean towards a more naturalistic subject."

"Now Kate," Pat chided, "We know for a fact that you were the principal photographer on that last nature film on the life of a raccoon. Your name is becoming very well known." He grinned, "Although I don't think most people fit the name with your ... er ... image?"

"Doesn't the name Ryan O'Hara conjure up a rugged conservationist, complete with a red, scraggly beard?" At their affirmative shake of their heads, "That's what I wanted," Kate laughed, "Now I ask you; would you hire me to camp out in the hills of a desolate mountain for two months in all kinds of weather?"

"Only if they'd seen you at the age of six being queen of the mountain!" Pat grinned, "How much time do you give to that old school of yours?"

"Not enough," Kate sighed. "There's always so much to do and never enough money to do it or enough hands. We're getting more and more kids who are having problems in an ordinary school, usually discipline but sometimes depression or withdrawal are symptoms of our kids, too. The Dominican Sisters who established the school are terrific. The classrooms are smaller than usual so that each student gets as much individual time and support as possible. The work is always uphill but when you finally reach them, and they really know that someone does care, it's all worthwhile." Kate's eyes were glowing with her enthusiasm.

"What exactly did you do in the school, Kate?" Leigh asked curiously.

"I work with individual kids, mostly from orphanages, they relate well with me because I've been there." She grew serious, "Not all kids are as lucky as I was to meet a family like the Ryan's." She paused, "I sometimes feel I need to do something to pay them back for letting me be a part of their family." She laughed, "Maybe I'll join a convent and become a real sister, and they already call me Sister Kate!"

"Is that what you want?" Pat asked, his eyes watching closely for her answer.

"No," Kate said quietly. "I've no calling. A convent isn't a place to hide from the world. I guess that's part of the problem. The sisters are so content and sure of their lives, I'm not." She smiled wryly, "I've always wanted to be a part of a family, my own, to have my own children, and to find someone who loves me enough to stay with me forever. Men don't seem to want permanent relationships anymore, present company excepted, of course."

"Of course," Pat agreed, "Don't worry Katie, I can't imagine you as an old maid, although being honest it's going to take someone special just to get the last word in!" He ducked to miss another pillow, this one hitting him squarely.

"Be nice to me, Pat," Kate warned teasingly, "I could get sick and stay home tomorrow."

"No way," he assured her, "You'll be there tomorrow, if I have to take you in your nightgown. As a matter of fact, that might be the way to start off a perfect working relationship with Morgan." he grinned wickedly.

Kate stood up, "True, but look what sleeping with her boss did for Leigh, she got a life sentence to you!" She walked to the door, "Good night Leigh and baby Ryan, see you in the morning, Pat." She went up the stairs humming, leaving Pat and Leigh smiling.

Once in her room, she closed the door. She put on a pale blue nightgown and lay down on the bed. Her forehead creased in the dark room. Her thoughts kept going back to the lonely years at the orphanage. Exhaustion finally claimed her, as sleep closed her eyes and relaxed her delicate features. Her heart shaped face, the small straight nose sprinkled liberally with freckles, and her long lashes resting against her cheeks, Kate slept.

CHAPTER 3

Kate awoke to the fresh smell of coffee and a gentle shake of her shoulder. She smiled at the young woman standing beside her bed, "Good morning," she said as she reached for the coffee. "What time is it?"

"Seven o'clock, Mrs. Ryan is still asleep, but Mr. Ryan left a note in the kitchen to please wake you at 7:00 sharp and give you this," she proceeded to hand an envelope to Kate. The maid grinned, "The coffee was my idea; if you need anything just tell me, my name is Mary."

"And mine is Kate, thanks for the coffee, I couldn't have done without it," Kate assured Mary as she slipped back through the door. Sipping the coffee, Kate opened her letter from Patrick.

'Katie,' it read, 'trouble at the plant, had to leave. Sleep in till 7, meet me at the office...take a cab on me ...address is 801 Market, by the Waterfront Renovation...See you at 9:00...Pat.'

Kate sighed. Trouble at the plant didn't sound good. Maybe it would help if I went in early. She grabbed her robe and went to the bathroom off her room, running a quick shower and shampoo, Kate was soon humming as she blew her russet hair dry. The natural curl framed her face and fell in soft waves to her shoulders. Picking a soft green pleated skirt and jacket and a ruffled print blouse, Kate was soon dressed and ready to go, grateful that her lashes and skin required little help in the way of makeup. She left a note for Leigh with Mary and called for a taxi. As she waited for her ride, Mary slid a tempting plate of scrambled eggs and bacon under her nose.

"Why Mary, how thoughtful! I'd love some breakfast, but I didn't want to bother you and to tell the truth, I'm not used to being waited on!" Kate exclaimed.

"No bother, Miss Kate. Sit down now and eat, I'll watch for your cab."

Kate finished just as the taxi arrived and hurried out the door. Breathing in the fresh early summer air, Kate smiled at the driver, "801 Market, by the Waterfront, please."

"Yes, ma'am," he grinned, his eyes noting her graceful walk and gentle warm smile.

The miles to the office were traveled swiftly as Kate watched the early morning traffic cruise past. She smiled at the familiar sights of St. Louis wondering how many of the busy motorists appreciated the tall gracious architecture of the passing buildings or the beautiful trees that lined the streets. Over the tops of the houses even from here, Kate thought, one could see the St. Louis Arch. It's glistening silver mirroring the sunlight as it stood six hundred feet above the city. It was a beautiful monument to the countless pioneers who set off from St. Louis to settle unknown land, a Gateway to the West. Flowing beside the Arch was the mighty Mississippi River, endless miles of twisting, turning water.

The screech of brakes threw Kate forward in her seat. "Looks like there's been an accident up ahead," her driver spoke, "are you all right?"

"I'm fine," Kate assured him. Reaching into her purse, she paid him, as she decided to see if she could be of help, more than able to walk the remaining blocks to the office.

Gently pushing her way through the small group of people, she found a dark-haired man leaning over the body of a woman; her hands were still tightly clasping her purse and her shopping bag, its contents spilling onto the pavement.

"May I help?" Kate asked, touching the shoulder of the man kneeling. His head turned, and for what seemed an eternity their eyes locked, a fathomless dark brown that held hers as a current seemed to flow between them. Stunned by the feeling, Kate shook her head. She turned her attention once again to the elderly woman on the ground. "What happened?' she asked, this time avoiding the dark compelling gaze of this stranger.

"She was crossing the street, an early morning motorist swung out and knocked her down, and he didn't stop." His voice was deep and sensuous.

Kate quickly felt for the woman's pulse as she had been taught when caring for Da, then gently checking her arms and legs for breaks.

"Have the police and an ambulance been called?" she asked, hoping her voice didn't sound as shaky as she felt.

"Yes, they have. Are you a nurse?" he asked.

Kate looked at the concerned faces around them; she started talking in German to them, at once eliciting a response as to who their victim was. "Her name is Ida Stocklin; she lives over the Donut Shop on Rivers. I've just sent someone to get her husband." She glanced up at the dark head beside her, startled to find a gleam in his eyes she could not understand. The sirens were heard as the police and ambulance arrived simultaneously, Kate stood up as Ida was lifted onto a stretcher, squeezing her hand and speaking softly to reassure her in her own language. The dark-haired stranger took charge of the authorities and filled them in on the circumstances of the accident and subsequent events. Ida's husband arrived seconds later and went with her to the hospital. Kate smoothed down her skirt and seeing the stranger still involved with the police, slipped unnoticed into the crowd and walked on towards the office on Market Street. Her senses still tingling from the dark brown eyes that had held hers for seconds etched across her mind, Kate wondered if she would ever discover who he was.

Arriving at the office minutes later, Kate admired the glistening shine of the buildings' walls. Like mirrors, the panels reflected the waterfront and the clear blue sky. Inside, she was directed to the top floor where the elevator took her to her destination in seconds. The doors opened to pale blue carpeting and cream-colored walls. The receptionist at the desk was a young man in his late twenties. His eyes flicked with interest at the small, shapely figure before him.

Kate smiled, "Mr. Ryan told to meet him in Mr. Buchanan's office at 9:00."

"Yes, ma'am," He said, "If you'll come this way, please." He led the way down the hall and opened the last door on the right it opened to a spacious room in different hues of blue and cream. It was a quiet, peaceful room. The atmosphere more of a gracious living room than an office. Kate sat down behind the desk. Might as well get myself situated, she thought, noting that the computer was a top of the line model. A copy/fax machine and a printer were located nearby. File cabinets were recessed into the wall. Kate opened the first drawer of her desk, the well-stocked supplies made her smile, I may never have to get out of my seat, she thought.

"What the hell do you think you're doing!" demanded a voice from the door. Startled, Kate looked up only to find her eyes locked by those same dark brown eyes from the accident. "You," he said cynically, "I might have known you knew who I was when you stopped to help. I must admit that was a novel approach, especially slipping away like that. My interest was caught. Too bad you didn't have the patience to wait a little longer before you followed up our-

-er... friendship." His eyes had narrowed, and his six-foot body was taut and tensed. A shadow passed his face for a moment, only to be replaced by an autocratic, almost ruthless stare. "Now would you please leave, or do I personally see you removed?"

For a moment Kate was stunned by the attack, but only a minute as realization of his speech hit home. She smiled suddenly at him and leaned back in her chair, relaxing her poise, watching him tense at her actions. "My, my, we are egotistical, aren't we," Kate said slowly, crossing her arms across her chest, "Is this how you lost your last four secretaries?"

"That is none of your business. Miss..." Morgan growled, his mood darkening by her apparent disregard of his commands.

"Now I wouldn't say that," Kate smiled, "who knows, Mr. Buchanan, this could be your lucky day!"

"...Only if you get out of it!" Morgan demanded taking a step closer to her seat.

"No," Kate corrected him, "only if you show a little patience and more civility. Your entire manner is very offending." Again, Kate smiled, her emerald eyes gleaming at his anger and relishing in knowing that Patrick would arrive at any minute.

"Why you ..." he took two more steps toward her only to be stopped by Patrick's cheery voice from the door.

"Hi, love! Sorry to keep you waiting... Morning, Morgan... Have you two met?"

"You know this pint-sized termagant?" Morgan growled.

"Temper, temper Mr. Buchanan." Kate responded, smiling at his confusion, "I keep telling you, it's in your best interests."

"You shut up!" Morgan demanded of Kate, her smiling mischievous eyes daring him to throw her out of the office.

"There's no need to get upset, Morgan," Patrick broke in, "There just isn't anyone else available. I called the agency this morning and they refuse to send anymore over."

25

"What did I tell you," Kate agreed cheerfully, "I'm your only hope ... Morgan." She playfully fluttered her long lashes at him.

Morgan looked from Kate to Patrick, he ran his hand through his black wavy hair. "Would somebody tell me what exactly is going on?"

"Sure ... Morgan, "Kate said smiling, "Meet secretary number five..."

"Is this some kind of a joke? Who the devil are you, one of Patrick's little people, no doubt?" Morgan asked sarcastically.

Patrick smiled, "I never thought of her like that, but it sure fits. Any pot of gold, if you're caught, Kate?"

"Now wouldn't you like to know, Pat me lad," Kate shot back talking in a thick Irish brogue. "Mr. Buchanan, I am Katherine or Kate if you prefer, sister of this young partner of yours. I've agreed to be a temporary secretary until you can hire another after this deadline is met."

"You're Pat's sister?" Morgan asked, his tone deadly quiet, "I will not be accused of nepotism. Thank you, Miss Ryan, but your, er...questionable services will not be required. Patrick, may I see you in my office, now please?"

"NO, I damn well won't" Patrick exploded. "You go through four secretaries in a matter of weeks, the service won't send anymore out. We need a secretary, a good one, Kate fits the bill and regardless if you do or don't like it, she STAYS! Not because she's my sister but because we have no other options available."

For a moment Patrick and Morgan flared at each other. If a fight were to result, Kate thought she'd put her money on Morgan. Although about the same height, Morgan's shoulders were wider, his jacket did not conceal his muscular arms and chest. Kate stood up, her movement causing both men to turn in her direction.

"Mr. Buchanan, I realize you are not thrilled with my presence. I have only to assume that my ...er...talents as a secretary are the major stumbling block. Would you agree to a week's trial?... It would give you a week to seek someone else, and I can either prove my capabilities or at the end of one week, I leave without pay." She met his gaze, not flinching from the animosity she saw reflected in their depths. "I will use my mother's name, O'Hara, my relationship with Patrick will not be mentioned ... "she paused, taking a deep breath, "Well, Mr. Buchanan... do I get that week's trial or not?"

Without a backward glance, he walked to his office door, "Be prepared for a long week... Miss O'Hara," he said as the door closed with a definite click.

For a moment there was silence, then Patrick turned to Kate, "Yes, I definitely think you should have worn a nightgown, Katie," he grinned, "I think Morgan would have been much more agreeable."

"Ah ... but what he'd have agreed to is another question!" Kate laughed, her husky chuckle filling the room with a contagious joy.

"Oh, Katie... Katie, I doubt this company or Morgan will ever be the same again." He walked laughing to the door, "I think Morgan will find it's a very long week, too!"

After he left, Kate looked at the pile of work already accumulated on the desk. Well, here goes, she thought and began typing silently. Only to be interrupted by the buzz of the intercom, "Yes, Mr. Buchanan?"

"I have some dictation, Miss O'Hara... You do take dictation, don't you?"

"I'll be right in." Kate flicked the switch. Knowing she was about to get a rapid-fire letter dictation unless she missed her guess, OK Buchanan, she thought, take your best shot.

Forty minutes later a tired but triumphant Kate sat back down, confident she had gotten every word correctly. By lunch, Kate had almost succeeded in catching up on the backlog of work. If I skip eating, she thought, I might just be able to get done by 5:00, better yet a sandwich and cold drink won't take but a minute and keep me on my toes for this afternoon. She called reception and asked for a sandwich to be delivered.

The pile dwindled all afternoon, by 5:30 Kate stood up and walked to Morgan's door; she knocked, and went in, carrying a stack or correspondence to be signed and sent out. Her desk was clear. Tomorrow would be just one day's work not two.

She carefully set the papers on Morgan's desk, "If you'll sign these, Mr. Buchanan, I'll send them out first thing in the morning. If there's nothing more, then ... Goodnight." Kate walked to the door, Morgan had not even looked up, and he gave no indication that he had even heard her.

As she reached the door, Morgan's voice broke the silence, "Did you know who I was this morning, Miss O'Hara?"

"No, "she paused, "not until you walked into this office." Kate responded, puzzled by the question. "Does that offend you?"

"Goodnight, Kate." Morgan answered, bowing his head back to his work. Kate walked out the door, only then remembering Morgan had not left for lunch either. She reached for the phone, ordered a couple of sandwiches and some coffee to be delivered and left the office.

Fifteen minutes later a knock sounded on Morgan's door. Impatiently Morgan walked to the door. "Yes, what is it now?"

"The sandwiches and coffee Miss O'Hara ordered for you sir."

"The what?" Morgan demanded as he opened the door.

"Miss O'Hara called down and asked for us to send out for some food for you, she said you'd skipped lunch and at the rate you were going would probably forget dinner, too."

Morgan took the food and closed the door, only then realizing he hadn't eaten all day. As he sat down to eat, he thought back to the strange red-haired vixen that had entered his office. What kind of a woman was she, he wondered, she stopped to help strangers, thought nothing of tangling with him, her emerald eyes still flashed before him, she was a damned good secretary if today's work was anything to go by, and she cared enough to see I had something to eat. He shook his head; we shall see... we shall see.

Kate arrived early next morning, feeling refreshed and ready to tackle the job at hand. By the time Morgan arrived, she had straightened the file system and had begun on the pile of work that had emerged overnight on her desk.

"Good morning, Mr. Buchanan," Kate said demurely, "Could I have a list of names you want me to put through by phone when they call and those you don't wish to be bothered with?"

"Certainly, Miss O'Hara," Morgan returned crisply, rattling off two dozen names in rapid succession, "those I'll see, the rest, take a number and I'll get back to them."

"As you wish, sir," she put down her pencil and resumed her typing glad she had had the foresight to pick up the pencil and paper when she did.

Morgan stood for a minute as if to speak, then walked briskly into his office.

The buzzer sounded frequently this morning, for files, for dictation, and for even more dictation. Kate did keep up with the pace, showing an outward calm, that seethed inside at the flow of work expected. Although to be honest, Kate thought, Morgan worked himself as hard or harder as he did her or anyone else. Lunch was another delivered sandwich, by late afternoon Kate was tired but triumphant that she had kept up. The phone rang just before 5:00. "R & B, Inc., may I help you?"

"Could be," said a familiar voice on the other end, "What can you do for me?' he added devilishly. Kate laughed, unaware that the sound was heard by Morgan. "We'll decide when you get home, and hurry I'm starved!"

"I'm on my way." Kate chuckled, putting down the receiver, surprised to see Morgan standing by his office door.

"Yes, did you want something?" Kate asked the twinkle still in her eyes from Danny's call.

"Keep the personal calls to a minimum, Miss O'Hara," he said crisply, "These are business phones and should not be tied up. Is that clear?" he demanded.

"Perfectly," Kate responded, her temper flaring briefly as her eyes clashed with his, aware of the powerful magnetism he held. The masculine, sensuality she felt whenever he was near. "Will that be all, Mr. Buchanan?" Kate added, hoping he would look away and not notice the trembling of her hands or her knees.

"Yes, Miss Ryan, for be it that your job should interfere with your love life." he said.

"Let me put your worries to rest then and assure you that it won't!" Kate retorted. "Goodnight!" She gathered her things and walked to the elevators, forcing herself to appear calm, just in case Morgan was watching. Oh, bother the man! Kate thought he will not ruin my evening; he will not make me lose my temper. He won't, he won't, he won't! By the time the elevator stopped on the ground level, Kate was in a much better mood and smiled at the guard standing at the entrance. "Goodnight, sir," Kate grinned, her hand touching a salute off her brow.

The guard grinned in return and tapped his heels together in answer to her salute, "Night, Miss."

Both laughed as Kate went through the door and walked the half block to the bus stop. The ride home to Pat's seemed short as Kate stepped off the bus only to be caught up in a burly hug by the youngest of the Ryan brothers.

"My turn," a second voice joined in, and a laughing Kate was passed to Mike and then Sean.

"What is this family reunion?" Kate asked, kissing each tall young man as they surrounded her.

"Actually," Danny began, "It's a kidnapping, you're being abducted and held for a king's ransom or a home cooked meal, whichever comes first."

"It had better be a meal," she said, "I just spent my last king's ransom on the bus ride!"

"Not you," Mike joined in, "where's your sense of fair play. The king--anxious to get his...wench...back, pays the ransom."

"And what if I don't know any kings?" Kate asked.

"Not to worry," Sean said, "We then go to rich, playboy bosses." his eyes dancing, "I hear you do have one of those ..."

"Fat chance!" Kate burst out laughing, "He's probably the one who staged the kidnapping in the first place to get me out of the office!"

Her brothers' joined in as they walked her home, each teasing and being teased in return. A happy group emerged on Leigh and Patrick.

"Get a move on, wench," Mike said, gently pushing Kate to the stairs, "You have ten minutes to make yourself presentable or..."

"Or what?"

"Or we, knights in shining armor that we are, find another wench to take to the ball," he finished, wickedly twirling his moustache.

"You're supposed to threaten her, not give her a reason to take her time!" Danny said, with mock concern.

Kate ran up the stairs, leaving them to their jokes. Exactly ten minutes later she returned, all eyes turned to stare as she descended down the stairs in a silver blue chiffon evening gown. Her hair was pulled up in a crown of soft curls, the halter bodice left her shoulders bare, her skirt a swirling mass of tiny pleats, she

31

seemed to float down the steps. "Well," Kate asked, the dimple appearing in her cheek, "Will this wench fit the bill?"

"Wow!" Sean said in answer.

"Holy cow!" was Mike's stunned reply. Danny said nothing, but he bowed low and extended an arm to Kate in invitation to join them. Even Patrick and Leigh were impressed by the picture of Kate. "You're beautiful, sis," Pat said, "almost as beautiful as my Leigh." He grinned, "You'll knock them for a loop at the club tonight."

"Thanks, Leigh, for the loan of the dress, or evening gown, whatever you want to call it. I can't say that I have a need for such clothes back in the Ozark Mountains. It's beautiful, and I feel like a princess wearing it. I promise not to let anything happen to it!" Kate told her as she passed.

"Don't worry about it; I'm certainly in no shape to wear it for quite some time. In fact, you should just keep the dress, it looks better on you than it ever did on me!" Leigh told her holding on to Pat's arm for balance.

Two cars were needed, and Kate was bundled into the front of Sean's, while the others were left to get in the back. Patrick and Leigh led the way.

CHAPTER 4

"Okay, Kate, now tell us how is Leigh, really?" Mike was suddenly serious, "We knew she was having trouble by Pat's letters but when we called, and Leigh said you were here, we figured it was a lot worse than anyone was telling us."

"You figured right, Mike." Kate said quietly. "Leigh's mother almost died having her, Leigh's problems are a repeat of the ones she had. Patrick is very much afraid for Leigh and their baby."

"Have you talked to the doctor?" Sean asked.

"Yes, before I came actually," Kate explained. "I had a letter from Pat, he unloaded. He was beside himself with worry. Unfortunately, he has to keep that worry from Leigh. He hired a nurse, to Leigh that nurse is a maid and cook, but Mary's a Registered Nurse, all the same."

"What can we do to help, Kate?" Danny responded for all three of them.

"Not much, unfortunately. We need to keep her spirits up and not tire her out but watch for any signs of unusual tiredness or pain. Other than that, we just sit back and wait like everybody else."

"So, the best thing we can do is to appear happy, keep things light, and not stay to make extra work for Leigh or the nurse?" queried Sean, his glance watching the face of Kate as she answered their questions.

"Right, I will keep you posted if there's any change, but for now there is nothing else." She sighed, "Sorry fellas'," then Kate grinned, "Unless you'd like to come to the office with me, then you could take over my job and I can stay with Leigh!"

"No chance!" Three voices chorused together. Sean laughed, "I would like to have the pleasure of meeting this Morgan, though."

"It's no pleasure, believe me!" Kate assured him, amidst the teasing of her brothers.

"Don't be too sure of that," Sean argued, "I'd just like to see all those sparks flying when you set him on his ear!"

"I don't do any such thing!" Kate denied huffily.

A loud guffaw from Danny brought fresh laughter, "Just what would you call your frankness then Kate? I can still hear you giving Ma and Da a once over for letting us in the creek, and that was twelve years ago!"

"It's not being frank; I was just ... stating facts!" By this time Kate was laughing too.

Sean pulled the car into the entrance of the beautiful Paledo Country Club. Gracious lawns surrounded the Colonial mansion as well as gardens of every flower imaginable. A lush greenhouse was hidden beyond the trees as well as a golf course and tennis courts. A huge glass dome housed an Olympic sized swimming pool that enabled its members to acquire year-round tans, the club itself, was a small palace of several restaurants and theaters.

The Ryan's elected to go Oriental and entered one of the club rooms called The Gardens. Japanese lanterns hung from the ceiling and a kimono covered waitress seated them at a table. Delicate hand painted china was set before them as they decided from the menu, each one determined to outdo the other.

Kate sat back and watched her family. So different, yet she thought, looking from one Ryan to the next. Pat, so blonde and blue eyed, like Ma. Sean was like Da, dark brown hair and eyes; he looked very dashing in his naval officer's uniform. Mike's moustache set his dark blonde hair apart from Pat; he was just finishing his internship at John Hopkins's Hospital in Maryland. And then there was Danny, she was roused from her musings by Sean as he pulled her to her feet.

"Wake up, Sis," he grinned, "Let's show these people how to dance." Together on the dance floor, Kate followed the intricate steps of Sean. As she laughed up into his dark face, she missed the startled eyes of her employer, seated In the corner of the room in a candlelit table for two.

Morgan caught the blur of a sliver blue dress, a crown of russet curls, and a familiar laugh. He watched as Kate whirled to the music, his face thoughtful as he studied them. He saw Sean hold her close and gently kiss her hair as the song ended. So, this was the man, who brought stars to her eyes, he thought wryly.

"Morgan, are you listening to me?!" A petulant voice interrupted his thoughts, "Why haven't you listened to a word I've said?"

He turned to look at the beautiful blonde seated opposite him, "Did you say anything I should have listened to, Marsha?" he asked, one brow raised in question.

"Now darling," the blonde answered, "you should listen to everything I say; I was just saying how interested Daddy's become in computers. You really should pay more attention to me."

"Oh?" Morgan queried, a cynical smile crossing his face as he watched Kate again appear on the dance floor, a smile that quickly turned to a frown as he saw her change of partners. Instead of the dark-haired naval officer, she was being held by a mustached blonde fellow, the waltz seemed to go on and on as she smiled warmly up into his face, they were deep in conversation as they passed his table.

"I want to get married, Kate ..." Morgan heard as Mike waltzed by... "You can stay in my apartment when you come to visit ..."

Morgan's eyes hardened as he watched Kate's silver silhouette disappear amongst the throng of people. "Are you ready to leave, Marsha?" he asked as he stood beside the table, the evening suddenly flat. "Because, I have had more than enough."

"But, Morgan ..." Marsha's sophistication floundered for a second at his autocratic manner. "We haven't even had one dance together..."

Morgan's face turned stony at her question, again seeing the silvery image of Kate in his mind. Damn Kate, he thought, how could anything she did outside of the office bother me? "Would you care to dance?" He asked Marsha stiffly, guiding the tall shapely body to the music. Her chatter soon stopped at his silent answers, and silently they moved across the floor. The music changed to a faster beat and before Morgan could escape the floor with Marsha, a laughing couple careened into them.

"Excuse us, please," a red-haired man said to Morgan. "She's always telling me I've got two left feet, but I like to drag her out on the dance floor anyway. Kind of keeps her on her toes, so to speak." He grinned apologetically. "I hope no damage was done ..."

For a second the dark brown eyes of Morgan's rested on Danny, a slight nod of his head to acknowledge the apology until he caught sight of Danny's partner ... Kate spoke first. "Good evening. Mr. Buchanan."

"Do you know this clumsy young woman?" Marsha's voice broke in. Still Morgan stared at Kate.

His face hooded as he finally spoke, "Marsha, permit me to introduce you to my new temporary secretary. Kate, this is Miss Marsha Adams-Smyth."

The aloofness and the strange vibrations that seemed to flow from this young girl to Morgan could almost be felt by everyone around them.

Kate's eyes flashed, "We have apologized Ms. Smyth ..." she began, her tone echoing the emerald glints.

"Adams-Smyth!" Marsha responded sharply, "If you can't even remember a simple name, no wonder Morgan only wants you as a temporary secretary."

Danny stepped in tactfully, "So you're Kate's boss, we were just discussing you earlier."

"Oh?" Morgan raised one eyebrow, and glared at Kate, "and what discussion was this?"

Kate grinned wickedly at Morgan and before Danny could stop her, "Why as to why I'm a temporary secretary, of course," she looked to Marsha, "I'm sure Morgan's told you all about it, hasn't he?" She saw Morgan's eyes gleam, as Marsha turned to look open mouthed at him. Morgan promptly disengaged Kate from Danny and quickly guided her to the floor before anyone could say another word.

"That was quite a feat," Kate grinned, "Was that to affect your rescue or to keep me from harm's way?" A quick look at Morgan's dark face, "No need to answer, I'd love to dance with you, Mr. Buchanan. Being temporary, this might be my only chance!"

"Do you always discuss business with your dates, Miss O'Hara?" Morgan rasped out, holding Kate even closer to his lean, hard body.

"Correction, Mr. Buchanan. We discussed you, NOT business. And to set your mind at rest, it was not in idealistic terms." Kate retorted, pushing in vain against his chest to gain some space.

"My error," Morgan answered primly, "Do you usually discuss other men with your legion of suitors? Is that how you keep them on their toes? A girl in every port? And while he's away at sea, another to take his place. This one seeks marriage, but no, that would cramp your style, so you just string him along. Is this last one the one you keep in reserve? I must say it's amazing how you can keep three on a string much less in one evening! Are they at three different tables and you having to keep shuffling from one to another?"

Morgan's speech caught Kate off guard, until she realized he had seen her with Sean and Mike as well as Danny. "No, actually, "Kate responded demurely, "they all get along famously and we're all at one table. It doesn't wear me out so much that way..."

"What kind of a woman are you?" Morgan demanded, "That it takes three men to satisfy you?" he paused, "But that's it isn't it?" He added softly, "You're not satisfied, always seeking one more to add to your collection."

"You don't associate with a very high class of people," Kate began, "if those are the kind you're used to. Although I'd say on second thought, your Ms. Adams-Smyth probably falls in that category. You do realize Morgan that we usually find what we look for?" she paused ignoring the anger in his face, "Do you see all the women you meet as conniving and greedy? Maybe unconsciously those are the kind you attract and settle for."

"Thank you, 'Dr. Freud' when I want analysis, I'll pay a shrink. Don't tell me that that's another of your many talents." Morgan's voice was clipped.

"To find those out, I'll have to be around for a lot longer than a temporary secretary. But that's all women will ever be for you. Just temporary! Unless, you start looking farther than your nose at the women around you, you'll never have anything else." Kate held her breath, knowing she had overstepped all boundaries.

For long moments, Morgan and Kate stared deep into each other's eyes. Anger replaced resolution. Morgan's eyes closed for a moment, when he opened them, they were hooded. He relaxed his hold on Kate, allowing her to draw apart from him. "I believe, Miss O'Hara that that was a challenge. Consider it accepted. You are no longer a temporary secretary. The job is yours for as long as you are capable of the task." He paused to rest steely eyes on Kate's delicate face, "But rest assured that I will not make life any easier for you. You will continue getting the same treatment you have received in the past, regardless of your relationship with my partner or me. Will you find a permanent job with R & B Enterprises to your liking or willit put a crimp in your ... er ... habits?"

"My ... er... habits are used to a permanent job, Mr. Buchanan. I will accept the offer of a longer stay at R & B, but it won't be permanent. After this contract is filled and after Leigh has her baby I will leave. I made a promise to someone and I keep my promises. Including the one I made to Patrick to stay."

Neither spoke for a few minutes, each deep in search of the other's motives and thoughts. It was Kate who broke the silence as she spoke somewhat hesitantly, "I believe our dance is over, thank you, but I need to get back to my...escort." Catching sight of Marsha's glowering stare, she added, "If looks could kill, you'd have to carry me off this floor in a coffin." She started to smile, the dimples appearing in her cheeks, a softness in her eyes.

Morgan grinned ruefully, "And who would carry me, Miss O'Hara? That look is directed at both of us ..."He paused, "Do you ever stay down for long, Kate?"

"Nope," she grinned, as they met Danny and Marsha, "Thank you for a most...enlightening...dance, Mr. Buchanan," Kate said.

"My pleasure, I assure you," Morgan responded smiling and with the same maneuver he had used on Kate, quickly had Ms. Adams-Smyth to the door.

An astonished Danny turned to Kate, "Are you sure you can handle him, Kate? I know I wouldn't like to encounter him as an opponent."

"But, Danny," Kate grinned, "We're on the same side, we both work for the same company!"

"Same company, maybe," Danny considered, "but Kate, my darling, don't underestimate him. From the sparks flying as you two were dancing, I would state unequivocally you are not on the same side. More like a head on collision. I just don't want you to be hurt and Morgan Buchanan is the kind of man who can hurt you."

"I'd need to care Danny to be hurt, and I won't make the error of caring about my boss, okay? So, stop worrying!"

"Kate, love, "Danny whispered in her ear as he steered her between tables to their impatiently waiting family, "You care about everyone and that is exactly what has me worried."

Sean's teasing interrupted them, as he noted that Kate could still walk back to the table despite dancing so long with his brother. Kate smiled and leaned back ln her chair. Kate could still feel the warmth of his body as he had held her close. Her skin still tingled where he had touched her.

CHAPTER 5

"I did not misfile the cost figures!" Kate's voice rose, as she stood rigidly before her boss.

"Then where, pray tell, have they disappeared to?" demanded a livid Morgan.

"Now calm down, both of you," Patrick spoke up. "They've got to be here someplace; files don't just get up and walk away."

"No," responded Morgan smoothly, "they probably had the help of my inept secretary."

"Those files were on my desk when I left for lunch." Kate bit back an angry retort but couldn't help adding. "And I am not inept!"

Two pairs of angry eyes clashed; Patrick shook his head in exasperation. Two weeks had passed, and an uneven truce had seemed to exist between his sister and partner. He was aware of the tension that seemed to always be present. For the life of him, he couldn't figure out why. If Kate was inept, as Morgan said, Patrick would have fired her himself. But on the contrary, she had done more work than her four predecessors combined. Very few people can keep up with the pace Morgan set. Kate kept up and still managed to appear calm and unhurried. Kate had never been known for a mild temper, Pat thought. But whenever Morgan was present sparks seemed to fly. Only last night, he remembered Kate telling

Leigh. She had never seen a man work so hard. It was almost as if Morgan were driven... Driven... That just might be the word to describe Morgan since Kate came. He worked long into the night. His temper was short and easily fused. He seemed to lose all patience with everybody.

Patrick sighed, maybe having Kate here in the office hadn't been the perfect solution. Maybe ... but until the baby came, this arrangement had to work out. Leigh was looking so relaxed now with Kate around. She didn't spend her time brooding. We're sure happy she's come back even if Morgan wasn't. The ring of the telephone broke into Pat's thoughts and the tension filled silence of Morgan and Kate.

"R & B," Kate responded automatically, she listened for a few seconds in silence, "Thanks, Rick, I'll deliver the message." She hung up the phone with a decisive click and spoke stiffly to Morgan, "A file was found by the janitor in the basement just a few minutes ago. That was reception, asking for confirmation that a Mr. Latham found the office."

"I don't remember having an appointment with a Mr. Latham..." Morgan began.

"That's because you didn't have one," Kate replied quietly. "See for yourself, the appointment book is open from twelve to one. Did you forget to tell me of a previous arrangement?"

"Can't you two stop bickering long enough to see what's happened?" Patrick exploded, "Doesn't it even matter that we've just encountered an industrial thief!"

Kate and Morgan turned to Patrick at the same time, Morgan was the first to speak, and "Industrial thief?" he asked, "hmmm... It would explain the missing file, the lunch appointment I never had."

"Not to mention a lot of other things around here," Pat interrupted, "All of those secretary's you went through, doesn't it occur to you that one of them could have been sent to us. Learn our layout, even get some of the information from our files and then quit, giving the same reason her predecessor gave. She fell for her boss."

"That hits the old ego hard," Kate said softly, "To think Morgan, you've been used. How unscrupulous..." Her words were so softly spoken, only Morgan heard them, he sent a dangerous glance at Kate, only to be interrupted by Patrick.

"I guess this puts Kate in the clear, I think you owe her an apology old friend," Patrick grinned. "I am glad to know she'll be around for a while. See you two later after you've made up." He walked out the door, only to stop and add, "I'll talk to security about appointments in the future, and anyone admitted will have to be checked out first, anything else?"

"I'll get back to you later on that," Morgan returned, his eyes hard, steely never leaving Kate's face.

"Right, then, I'll meet you by the car Kate in fifteen minutes to go home," and he was out the door.

"You won't be meeting Pat as arranged," Morgan said quietly.

"On the contrary," Kate retorted, "I will be, there's not enough work left to do to keep me overtime."

"Patrick said to apologize, instead we'll go out to dinner, where we won't be interrupted, I have a few things to say..."

"If that's an invitation," Kate said, "Sorry, Mr. Buchanan, I refuse. I see quite enough of you during office hours without adding more." She smiled mischievously, ignoring the warning signals of anger surrounding Morgan. "So, it did rankle, not only were you wrong about my capabilities but possibly about another employee as well. Tsk... Tsk... two errors in one day..."

Morgan's hands were like iron bands on Kate's arms as he drew her to his hard-masculine body. Kate pulled in her breath sharply, raising startled yet defiant eyes toward his, steeling her nerves and senses that were playing havoc with his nearness. Dancing close to him was nothing compared to the onslaught of emotions coursing through her body. Her knees were weak, her stomach in knots as she dared him with her eyes to let go of her arms.

"Go out with me Kate," Morgan said softly, his voice husky. "I know you're not immune to me, I can feel you tremble in my arms when I danced with you. Now as I hold you close ... "He didn't need to finish; Kate was all too aware of how she reacted to his touch.

"No, Morgan, I'm not immune to your charms." Kate said hesitantly, afraid to speak her thoughts, "But I won't go out with you. We come from two different worlds. What we want from life doesn't even come close. The less we see of each other the better." She tried to push him away only to find him an impenetrable wall. "How does the saying go? Don't mix business with pleasure... "

"What we want from life?" Morgan echoed softly. "I want a russet haired elf whose waist I can span with my hands... Whose emerald eyes taunt me ... " His hands slowly left her shoulders to encircle her arms, he drew her trembling body closer still to his. His lips touched hers with a featherlike caress.

Kate moaned, "No, Morgan, please ..." she whispered, only to be silenced by the hungry possession of her lips by Morgan's. At his touch, Kate's body seemed to melt into his. Slow delicious warmth stole through her, as Morgan's lips left hers only to return as if drowning seeking more.

Kate's arms went up Morgan's chest and slowly circled his neck, her fingers lost in the thick curl of his hair. Her body seemed to mold itself against Morgan's as he crushed her slight form against his. The sharp shrill ring of the telephone broke into the silence of the room.

"Let it ring," Morgan moaned huskily as his lips traveled slowly across Kate's face ... Kate shook her head, and with trembling hands picked up the telephone.

"R & B, may I help you please?" She kept her eyes averted, not daring to look at Morgan." One moment, please." Kate said softly, "It's for you, Mr. Buchanan... a Mr. Adams-Smyth seeking confirmation on your dinner date. It seems his daughter forgot the time." For a moment, Kate raised her glance and looked deep into the hooded dark gaze of Morgan, her own eyes suddenly bright with unshed tears.

"Kate... I" Morgan began huskily reaching once again for her. She shook her head, carefully managing to avoid touching his hands as she walked quickly to the door.

"Have a nice evening, Morgan," Kate whispered at the door and managed a weak smile, "You were saved by the bell," she blinked hard, fighting for control, "Consider the apology accepted... It's better for both of us this way, friends, not lovers ..." she said softly as a solitary tear fell slowly down her cheek. Without another word, she left, leaving Morgan standing by her desk, his face a mask.

Reluctantly he picked up the phone, "Hello, Mike... Buchanan here ... Well I think Marsha made an error in the date... That's right... we had no dinner date for this evening...thanks Mike...Some other time would be fine... I'll give you a ring..." With a heavy click, Morgan hung up the phone. His thoughts wondered back to only minutes before when he had held Kate in his arms. He could still feel the velvet softness of her skin against his hands, the slight scent of her perfume still remained. Morgan stared into the empty room for long minutes. His face becoming determined, he rose and with decisive movements walked out the door, locking each behind him.

Kate was quiet on the way home with Patrick. Her face turned toward the windows to avoid conversation. Her mind was whirling with a mass of conflicting emotions. She cared for Morgan. God help me, but he holds a powerful magnetism that she was finding increasingly hard to fight against. He was infuriating, Kate smiled, he certainly wasn't boring to be around. Their discussions were a tug of war between their wills. Kate sighed, she could picture him dancing with Ms. Adams-Smyth, and pain stabbed her heart at the thought of Morgan with someone else.

Kate chose to sit back and listen to her brothers' noisy exchange at dinner. Tonight was their farewell. Mike, Sean, and Danny were leaving in the morning, each to their respective jobs, confident that Leigh was in good hands with Kate.

"Well, Mike," Sean asked, "When do we meet this girl of your dreams?"

"I can't imagine any girl willing to take you on for life, better have her head examined at that hospital of yours!"' Danny put in.

"What's her name?" Patrick joined in, "She does have a name, I take it?"

"Her name is Katrina, I call her Kat for short,"' Mike answered, taking the teasing in stride, "and she knows what she's taking on, her father was a doctor, is I should say, and Kat is a nurse at John Hopkins. Medicine has always been there. She's quite a girl."

The doorbell rang, and Patrick rose to answer it, surprised to find Morgan, "Come in Morgan, is there trouble at the office?" Pat asked remembering the scene earlier.

"No, no not that I know of... I needed to talk to Kate."' His face was set, his jaw tense, "Is she here?"

"Yes," Pat answered warily, "Right through those doors, she's with our ..."

Morgan didn't wait; he walked right in, only to stop in midstride. Kate stood on tiptoe; kissing the tall blonde-haired man with a moustache he had seen her with at the Paledo Country Club. It was evident a toast had just been made.

"Morgan," Leigh cried joyfully, "Come in, we just heard some terrific news. There's finally going to be a wedding in this family! Mike and Kat are getting married!"

Morgan's eyes seemed to bore through Kate. For long seconds their eyes clashed and held a battle of wills and thoughts. Kate was surprised when Morgan had walked in, even more so by the anger and animosity she saw in him. It was Kate who looked away first, still puzzled as to what could have made Morgan so angry.

"Congratulations," Morgan said woodenly, "I won't disturb you or intrude on a family affair." He walked quickly to the door.

"But Morgan," Leigh called after him, "what brings you here this time of night?"

Morgan stopped and looked directly at Kate, his eyes hard and his voice remote, "It wasn't anything important," He hesitated, it's better this way, right Miss O'Hara?"

Kate slowly shook her head, unable to utter a sound. Without another word, Morgan left. The family stared in puzzlement at the closed door. "What was that all about?" Sean asked, breaking the silence, as everyone started talking at once. Only Danny was silent watching Kate.

With the help of makeup, Kate arrived at work next morning her sleepless night successfully hidden. She dreaded going into the office, afraid of what to expect after last night. At the door, Kate took a deep breath and walked in relieved to find it empty. On her desk was quickly written note ... 'Business with Halloran in New York. Return on Friday of next week. Cancel appointments. Papers will arrive by courier. Signed simply, 'M'.

Kate sighed, relieved to get a breathing space from Morgan. In the week before he came back, she could rebuild her defenses get herself under control. Shaking her head to clear it, Kate started to work.

The week seemed to drag, each time the phone rang. Kate hoped yet dreaded that it might be Morgan. Each morning the courier arrived with another package of work and left with the previous days. Kate was disappointed when there was no note from Morgan, other than instructions. She assumed Patrick spoke to him, both avoided mentioning his name to the other, Patrick to avoid any sparks in the lull and Kate to avoid any pain.

Friday morning dawned with an overcast sky of heavy dark rain clouds. The very air seemed oppressive as stillness blanketed the area. Kate woke with a dull headache; her first thought was of Morgan's return today. Anticipation mixed with dread and fear, Oh God! Kate took a deep breath. Don't let him shatter my newly built defenses! She groaned as she rose from the bed. A half hour later found her downstairs in a pale-yellow pantsuit, a delicate flowered blouse clinging to the soft curves of her body. Her hair was feathered gently back from her face. Kate was nervous and unsure. Calling a cab, she left a note for Patrick with Mary telling him she'd meet him at the office.

As she opened the door and an empty desk awaited her. Kate let out a long breath, only to catch it as Morgan stood in the dark doorway. His face hidden by the shadows, she didn't see the light appear in his eyes as he watched her enter or hear his quick intake of breath as sunshine seemed to fill the room.

For long minutes, Kate stared at the shadowy figure, trying desperately to appear calm.

She cleared her voice, "Good morning," Kate said softly, hoping it sounded normal.

Morgan inclined his head slightly, "Morning" he responded. His voice clipped.

"How was your trip?"

"Uneventful."

"Does that mean it was successful?"

"Successful? How do you define the word success? Profitable? Rewarding?" he paused. "What does success mean to you, Kate?"

Kate hesitated. "I think success ...is a way to judge how close a person comes to reaching or exceeding his own goals or expectations."

Morgan took a step forward, "Then by your definition my trip was successful, Miss O'Hara. It's strange that your terms didn't include any mention of profit or money. Surely success is equated with how rich a person is?"

"Do you judge a person by his wallet, Morgan?" Kate asked, "If a man sets a goal to remaining dependent from all others. He grows his own food, makes his own clothes, etcetera. He has no money, in fact he has very little of anything. Yet, he's done what he's set out to do. That man is successful. Being successful doesn't have anything to do with riches."

"Is being a philosopher another of your ... dubious ... talents?"

"You asked what I thought," Kate said, puzzled by his aloofness. "I simply answered."

"So, I did" he paused, "I believe there's work to be done. Miss O'Hara. I ...

"Morgan!" Patrick grinned as he entered the room.

"Patrick." Morgan said, shaking his head ruefully. "Come in. I'll fill you in. Halloran said ...." he and Patrick disappeared behind his office door.

Kate took a deep breath and sat down, glad for the support to her shaking knees and trembling hands. Seconds later she started slowly typing the papers Morgan had placed on her desk earlier.

When the phone rang, Kate jumped, surprised at the quick passage of time..." R & B... Yes Rick... send her up ... believe me she's got clearance." Kate grinned as Leigh was escorted to the door. "Thanks, Rick; I'll see she gets to Mr. Ryan's office." With a last backward glance, Rick walked back out the door.

"Who does he think I am?" Leigh whispered loudly, "I've never been looked at so suspiciously in my life! What does he think I'm carrying? A bomb? These maternity clothes are just camouflage?"

Kate giggled, "He probably thought you were smuggling spies."

"Now I ask you, Kate," Leigh tries to look serious, "do I look dangerous to you?"

"Only to a nervous stork!" Kate responded. "What brings you to R & B? Not planning on returning to work, are you?"

"You're safe; I don't think my fingers could reach the keys anymore!" Leigh flinched.

Kate spoke calmly, "Are you okay?"

"I'm fine," Leigh said, her eyes closed, then opened to meet Kate's, "Just very pregnant. I'm sure everybody; everybody pregnant that is, feels the same way! It was just a twinge, nothing to worry about."

"Have you had these before?"

"No...At least not before today, don't look so worried Kate." Leigh said quietly. "Nothing is going to happen to me or my baby. More than anything else I want to have Pat's baby and shower love on both my husband and child." A wry laugh escaped her lips. "Quite a change isn't it, Kate. I was the career woman who knew it all. Then I met a young, very broke young man and promptly fell head over heels in love with him! Of course, I worked my fingers to the bone trying to get him to notice me!" She patted her swollen middle lovingly. "He did notice me, didn't he little one?" She raised somber, thoughtful eyes to Kate," Kate... if... "She stopped, only to continue." If anything should happen to me, would you let Pat know that he's the best thing that's ever happened to me." Continuing, regardless of Kate's interruptions. "Let him know, how very much I love him and have always done ..." Seeing the importance of this to Leigh.

Kate shook her head solemnly. "I promise but you tell him. He's just in the office with Morgan... "

"Kate." Leigh flinched again her face suddenly pale. "I think you'd better get Pat ..." Suddenly Leigh slumped in her chair. Kate moved quickly, hitting the intercom buzzer as she rounded the desk to catch the heavy burden of Leigh.

"Yes ...Miss O'Hara?" Morgan's voice sounded from the intercom.

"It's Leigh...Pat... Morgan...Come quickly!" Kate gasped, her small frame supporting Leigh's weight from falling. Her words were barely uttered when both men arrived through the office door. Pat's ashen face as he saw Leigh tore at Kate's heart. She missed Morgan's intake of breath as he saw Kate under the strain of holding up the dead weight of the unconscious Leigh. Patrick and Morgan carefully lowered her to the floor. Released from the weight Kate's knees buckled, only to be caught by Morgan as she slid down beside Leigh.

"You little fool," he said under his breath, "You're no match to catch her."

"I'm alright...really... I'm stronger than I look...!" Huge emerald eyes caught Morgan's. Her body still trembling, Kate took Leigh's pulse. Rising up on unsteady legs, she crossed to the phone and instructed reception to get an ambulance for Mr. Ryan's wife. Pat seemed to be in a trance, his eyes never leaving Leigh's face.

Shaky hands dialed home, "Mary? ...This is Kate...Leigh's just collapsed...She's still unconscious ... Only once ... I questioned her about it, she said only a few times today... okay... ambulance is on its way... right ... meet you there."

Kate took a deep steadying breath, "Morgan, we need to get her legs up slightly and cover her for shock. A damp rag would be helpful in bringing her around," she sighed, "I don't think Pat's going to be any help at all ... We were just talking about if anything should happen to her ... " Kate's voice shook unsteadily.

Morgan's finger gently lifted Kate's chin, his lips brushed her forehead in reassurance, "She'll make it, Kate." he whispered.

Kate squared her shoulders, "Right," she whispered. In unspoken accord they raised Leigh's feet and covered her with both Pat and Morgan's jackets. Kate's handkerchief was dampened, and she sponged Leigh's face and wrists. After what seemed an eternity, Leigh moaned and opened her eyes.

"Leigh... "Pat whispered hoarsely.

"Don't move, Leigh," Kate broke in softly, her voice steady, "an ambulance is on its way. Are you in any pain?"

"My...back...hurts...is ...my baby...alright?"

"You'll both be fine. But it's very important that you don't try to move. Do you understand?" Kate asked urgently.

"Yes ..." she swallowed, "Pat?"

"Yes, love, I'm here. Don't talk, save your strength. Please ..."

The shrill ring of the phone broke into the tense room. Morgan answered, taking charge of the situation, "Send them up, and then keep the elevators clear. The ambulance is here, Kate, "Morgan said, "You and Pat go with Leigh. I'll clear up the confusion here and be in later." He paused, "unless you'd like me to go with you now?" His look seemed to hold a question Kate didn't understand.

"Thanks, Morgan, once we get her to the hospital, we'll be fine. You go ahead and stay here." Kate looked away hoping Morgan wouldn't see how much she wanted him to go with them, how very much she needed him.

"Right." Morgan said flatly, turning to allow the paramedics entrance.

CHAPTER 6

Kate stood by the window of St. Luke's Hospital, looking out over the bustling traffic of the St. Louis streets. She sighed, her hand rubbing softly against her temples, the strain of the last few hours taking their toll. Leigh had remained conscience on the way to the hospital. Her doctor had met them, as well as Mary, an emergency Caesarean had followed. Kate and Pat waited anxiously by the operating doors, neither daring to speak, each afraid to voice the danger that Leigh and their baby were in.

Morgan's footsteps sounded ominously down the corridor, his eyes traveling first to Pat's drawn face and then to linger on Kate's dark shadowed eyes. His eyebrows rose questioningly for any new.

"She's in the operating room," Kate spoke breaking the silence, "they're doing an emergency C section."

"It's my fault," Pat said flatly. "If anything happens to Leigh it'll be my fault."

"Why," Kate asked, "Because you love her?" She shook her head and knelt beside her distraught brother. "Oh, Pat, don't you see? Leigh wanted this baby even more than you did. It was a way she could show you how much she loves you. This baby, your baby will be a sign of the happiness and joy you've shared." She paused searching for the right words, hoping Pat could understand. "Just before ... Leigh collapsed she asked me to tell you something, if anything should happen to her ... she said to tell Pat that he's the best thing that's ever happened to me and tell him not to worry, that she knows that she and the baby will be alright ... Pat ... trust her ... she knew the chances she was taking... she knew but she chose, you both chose to have this baby." She watched Pat closely, forgetting Morgan or the hospital.

"Mr. Ryan?" the doctor spoke from the door.

"Yes?" Pat looked up.

"Congratulations, sir, it's a girl. Both are doing just fine. It was touch and go for a little while, but your wife and daughter just wouldn't give up. That's quite a family you've got."

Relief flooded Pat's face; he shook the doctor's hand, a smile covering his face, "Thank you ... thank you..."

Tears were streaming down Kate's face; her shoulders shook as Morgan gently pulled her to him and held her. His hands brushing back her hair. Kate cried her relief, "They're all right ... Oh, thank God ..." She didn't feel Morgan brush a kiss across her hair. His arms seemed a haven of strength when Kate finally raised her head, she smiled shyly up at Morgan. "I got your shirt all wet... Did he really say they're both alright, Morgan? ... Where's Pat?"

Morgan smiled, his eyes glowing with warmth. "In answer to your questions, I don't care about the shirt, yes they're really alright and where do you think? He's with Leigh and his new daughter, all six pounds and three ounces of her." He gently wiped the last remaining tears from her face. "Would you like to take a peek at her? I understand we are to be her godparents."

"Could we?" Kate asked, her eyes bright, suddenly very conscience of Morgan's arms around her. She licked her lips nervously. Morgan's arms tightened.

"We can," He murmured huskily, "just as soon as I congratulate her godmother." His lips descended upon hers, gently searching, seeking her response. Kate's body responded without

54

thought. Her hands crept up to circle his shoulders and lose them in his hair..." Kate ..."Morgan whispered as he kissed her again, "We have to stop this,"

"I know... "Kate said softly, her hand gently touching Morgan's cheek, she smiled tremulously, "Let's go see baby Ryan, my friend."

Arm in arm they walked down the hall and to the nursery. The glass covered walls showed six tiny little incubators. Each complete with a perfect baby.

"They look so small," Kate said, "Can you see which one is Leigh's?"

Morgan's deep chuckle, "Well, if I had to make a guess, I'd say she was the second one in, I think she's going to look like her aunt," With that he pointed to a small bundle, oblivious to the noise around her. Her tiny head covered with small wisps of strawberry blonde hair. At his tap at the window, the nurse attending the babies looked up and smiled, especially when Morgan pointed first to Kate's glowing mane and then to the baby's. She wheeled the tiny bed to the window, so they could have a closer look. At the foot of her bed was a tiny card reading Baby Girl Ryan.

"Isn't she beautiful," Kate spoke with awe, "so tiny, so perfect ..." The tears returned to her eyes, "How could anyone not want .... She shook her head and added, "One of their own?" Kate blushed, caught unaware by the question that seemed to be hidden within the question. "I'd like a houseful," she answered, her eyes resting on the tiny form, "but for right now," she grinned, "I'll just have to be content to be Aunt Kate and spoil her shamelessly," she looked up at Morgan, "Do you like children?"

"As long as they're someone else's," he added.

"You don't want any of your own?" Kate watched his face, hurt by the thought that he could be so cold.

"Kids come into the picture, things change, they're ok for some people, Pat and Leigh for instance, but not me." Morgan's voice was flat. Kate wondered at the hurt she felt she heard in his voice, puzzled by his certainty. Both were startled by Pat's cheery voice as he enveloped Kate in a bear hug.

"Isn't she the most gorgeous baby you've ever seen?" He swung Kate around, "Leigh is doing fine, just tired," Pat stopped to look at his daughter, "She's sleeping, she has the most beautiful smile on her face, just like the one Leigh has," His fingers touched the window, talking more to himself than to Morgan or Kate, "Hair the color of burnt gold, Leigh's mouth, she is so perfect," He paused, "things will never be the same again," Startled Kate looked up at Morgan and then to Pat," I don't think, " he continued, " I'll never be able to look at Leigh or my daughter again and not remember how close I came to losing the most important things in my life, Everything else seems to fade away as insignificant, the house, the job, everything, Our family is complete, love has brought us full circle," He grinned, "Sorry, I'm babbling just wait until you have one of your own, you'll see., "

"By the way," Morgan's deep voice seemed to echo, "I never did get to tell you congratulations," His hand grasped Pat's, "What are you going to name her?"

Pat couldn't stop smiling, "After her grandmother and the person who saved her life, Katherine Anne," He saw the look of surprise on Kate's face, "Without you, half-pint, Leigh would have lost the baby. You stayed calm while I proceeded to fall apart. If she had moved, the placenta could have detached." He paused, "Leigh would have died from hemorrhaging, Oh Kate...I love you; I thank God for ever sending you to the Ryan clan." Tears fell unheeded down their faces as Kate and Pat blocked out the world ...Morgan stood by deep in thought his glance never leaving Kate's face.

Kate woke up; memories of yesterday's miracle brought delicious warmth to her. Stretching slowly, she turned over, only to stare for a second at the clock beside her. It can't be that late! Morgan will kill me, she thought, as she flew to the shower. Twenty minutes later, Kate ran out the door to the waiting cab. Morgan had a thing for punctuality, Kate didn't want to spoil the sense of friendship that had seemed to blossom through yesterday's ordeal.

As the cab raced toward downtown St. Louis, Kate remembered the ecstatic words of her brothers over the new arrival. Mike it seemed had an arrival of his own; Katrina had consented to marry him. He had promised to bring her home with him for the Baptism. I hope he'll be as happy as Pat and Leigh, Kate prayed, wondering if she would ever be that happy.

Kate paid the driver and ran through the doors, not noticing the quiet that lay like a blanket around her. Reaching her office, she almost collided into Morgan as she dashed through the door.

"Oh, Morgan," Kate blurted, "I'm sorry I'm late. I overslept. I won't let it happen again ... I promise!" She looked up at him, instead of the scowl she thought would be there, Kate was surprised to find him smiling.

"Kate," he began, "you can't be late when you're not even supposed to be here."

Traveling backwards, Kate remembered the quiet of the outer offices. "It's Saturday," she replied meekly. "I came to work on Saturday!" Kate sat down, angry at how stupid she felt she must look to Morgan. She looked up at a grinning Morgan, "and what reason do you have for being here today?"

"I didn't get much done yesterday, there's a lot of work, or rather loose ends from that trip to tie up. I figured today was as good a day as any."

"Would you like some help?" Kate offered.

"...On Saturday?" Morgan asked, surprised.

"Well as long as I'm here, you might as well put me to work," Kate grinned, "But since it is Saturday, I expect to finish early. Let's get cracking Mr. Buchanan," Her eyes twinkling as she started sorting the work on her desk, softly humming to herself.

Morgan stood and watched Kate for a moment, the sunlight through the window catching her hair and making it glow. She failed to see the look of admiration that entered his eyes as he turned and entered his own office.

Together they worked for almost four hours. Companionably, they sorted out and tied up the orders and cost figures Morgan had drawn up. As she put away her supplies, Kate glanced up at the clock, surprised to find it already past one o'clock. Lunch! She decided; her body suddenly hungry. She glanced at Morgan's door, he hasn't eaten either, she thought. Dare I suggest we get a bite together? At a restaurant of my choosing, she grinned and made a quick phone call before she picked up her tote bag. Tentatively she knocked on the door, "Morgan?" Kate began, not wishing to interrupt if he were still busy.

"Yes, Kate," Morgan answered, "Problems?"

"No, I just finished the last of it, I was wondering," she paused, "if you'd like to have a bite to eat?"

Morgan looked up, "My treat," Kate continued, "You've heard the old saying, all work and no play makes Morgan a ... tired," as she noticed how dark his eyes seemed to be, "and dull boy!" she finished.

Morgan stood up and flexed his arms; the tension from bending over his desk all morning seemed to weigh him down. Some of the tiredness seemed to leave him, as he smiled, "You did say this lunch was on you, right?!"

"Right," Kate grinned mischievously, "It's a very casual place," She walked over to him, and untied his tie. His closeness made her hands tremble slightly. She looked up, "You can leave your jacket here," and she moistened her lips, "roll up your sleeves " When he didn't move but just seemed to stare at her, his eyes half hidden by his lashes, "Please?" Kate added suddenly unsure of herself.

"Casual?" Morgan asked, his brows rising to question Kate. "So be it." As he began to roll up his sleeves, he answered, "Okay, Kate lead on to this 'casual' place."

"You'll love it," Kate said hurriedly her breath catching, "It has a very different ...atmosphere ... so, to speak."

Going down the elevators, Morgan crossed his arms and studied Kate, "Does this restaurant have a name, Kate?"

"Oh, yes," Kate answered avoiding his eyes, "but I won't tell you, it would spoil the surprise."

"Will we need a car or is it within walking distance?" he asked.

"No," Kate answered as they reached the front doors, laughing at Morgan's confusion. "Just trust me, okay?"

"Now that's asking a lot, he said his voice serious, "women aren't to be trusted."

"Most women," Kate countered. "Surely from your vast experience of women there have been a few that you could trust?"

"Very few," Morgan said cynically.

"Okay then," Kate said stubbornly, "Don't trust me. Just don't ask any questions, at least not for now ... or is that too much to ask?"

"That I think I can manage, after all I'm almost twice your size and well able to take care of myself."

A grin escaped Kate's pleading face, "Don't let my size fool you, Morgan, under this five feet two frame lies a black belt in Judo. So, either you come willingly, or I shall just proceed to take you against your will." The thought of Kate doing anything against Morgan's size and bulk was ludicrous and both burst out laughing.

"I don't know if I believe that Judo business, but if it means that much to you, I'll follow wherever you lead, no questions asked. Will that do?" Morgan grinned.

"I guess it'll have to," Kate murmured trying to still her twitching lips. Looking around the busy street, she waved as she spotted the young man coming towards them.

"Here we go, boss," Kate giggled, "all aboard the O'Hara Express." Kate's friend walked a bicycle built for two to Morgan's surprise. "I get fronts, since I know the way, since you're such a big strong man you're in the back where the power lies." She paused, "Okay?"

"You're crazy Kate ... but you're on. By the way, I now know why you asked me to lunch, Red!" Morgan smiled and this one reached his eyes. "You just wanted pedal power!"

Kate laughed; her joy contagious. "You think you've got me all figured out, don't you?" She turned to the young man who'd brought the bike, "Thanks Paul, we'll bring it back when we're done. Okay?"

"Pop said to keep them as long as you want," Paul smiled anxiously at Kate, "Anything Sister Kate wants, she can have!"

"Start pedaling Morgan, you're going to earn this lunch!" Kate tossed her tote bag in the basket on the front of the tandem. The first few blocks were wobbly to say the least, but as they turned left on Sixth Street, they had achieved harmony. Kate looked back, her eyes shining, the wind blowing her hair into her face. "You're not bad," she paused, "for a city slicker."

"You'll eat those words. O'Hara." Morgan threatened playfully.

Kate guided them to Farmer's Market off the waterfront. Bicycling between the many stands of produce and the throngs of shoppers took all Kate's concentration but she still managed to wave to several friends as they called her name. A small ten-year-old girl stood at the rear entrance holding out a basket, as they went by Kate grabbed the basket without stopping. "Thanks. Maria!" she called.

"Anything else you want, Sister Kate?" the young girl asked running beside the bike.

"Not a thing, it smells 'mucho bene' Maria, tell your Papa thanks very much."

She waved at Maria and several other dark-haired children beside her. Kate directed them past the hospitals on Kings Highway and into Forest Park.

When St. Louis was only just beginning to grow into a metropolis, someone had the foresight to keep the country even within the city. One thousand three hundred acres in the center of St. Louis were an invitation to the millions of residents to enjoy tree lined walkways, boating lagoons, and picnic areas. Hidden away in the lush green of the park was the St. Louis Zoo, the Jewel Box featuring flowers from all over the world, and the Planetarium. Kate threw back her head, luxuriating in the feel of the wind and the breath of clean cool air, aware as never before of the stifling confines of an office. She braked before one of the lagoons, under a tree she spread a blanket from the basket and handed a somewhat stunned Morgan an Italian beef sandwich and a glass of wine both of which came from the mysterious basket.

Morgan dropped onto the blanket, his hand brushing his hair back from his eyes. "I like your taste, Kate," he smiled, breathing deeply of the grass and the trees. He watched ducks swim in the cool, clear water. "Will you tell me the name of your restaurant now?"

"It's my Oasis," Kate replied, pleased that he liked her surprise. "Whenever I start to feel the walls closing in, this is where I come. It reminds me of home, gives me time to think and just relax." She took a bite of her sandwich, "The food is from Mario's, Maria's father is from Italy and when he come to the United States, he brought his recipes. If you love these, you should try his lasagna, it's out of this world!" She rolled her eyes, suddenly a little self-conscience of her disheveled hair. "I guess... this is a change from your usual luncheon dates."

Morgan's hearty laugh made Kate smile, "You could say that, Red! Going to a restaurant all the time, all of them requiring a tie of course, I guess you could even call them stuffy." He stopped, "Am I stuffy, Kate?" he asked suddenly.

"No, you are not under any conditions!" Kate replied quickly, putting his mind at rest. "But you did look tired, I wondered if some fresh air would help you? With your tan, I didn't think you were used to spending so much time indoors as you have been lately."

Both finished eating in companionable silence, content to watch the people around them. Kate watched a young couple rowing unsuccessfully around the lagoon; she turned to Morgan, only to find his eyes closed. He looked younger when he was asleep, and even vulnerable, she resisted the impulse to brush his hair back from his forehead. The laughter of children from a nearby fountain caught her interest. She took her tote bag from the bicycle basket and took out one of her cameras. She began to photograph without a glance at the curious bystanders who stopped and watched. On the way back to the blanket, Kate couldn't resist taking a few pictures of Morgan as well. She put her camera carefully away and fed the ducks patiently waiting for Morgan to wake up.

When he did, it was to the sound of excited children's voices. All of whom seemed to be talking at once to a relaxed Kate sitting Indian style on the grass.

"... On the count of three, lay back. Ready? One ... two ... three ... what do you see?" she asked softly.

"A mountain ..."

"That's a dragon!"

"A lion..."

"Soldiers!"

"A unicorn!"

Came the excited replies as Morgan joined them, silence grew heavy. "What are you doing?" he asked Kate.

"It's called cloud watching. Didn't you ever watch the clouds and imagine all sorts of images up in the sky when you were little?" Kate replied.

"No." Morgan replied solemnly.

"Well there's no time like the present to learn." Kate said briskly, catching a glimpse into a lonely childhood. "Lie back." she directed. "Look at the white puffy clouds. Imagine them as being something else, are they in the shape of anything? Look over there; see the mane on that lion?"

"Show him the unicorn!" the children began.

"He'll find them himself," Kate replied, watching Morgan study the wispy forms. She raised a finger to her lips to quiet the voices and whispers.

"It looks like a giant … computer!" Morgan began.

Kate covered her face with her hands, "You're hopeless!"

"Alright, I'll try again," He chuckled squinting his eyes. After several minutes, he pointed to a cloud saying softly, "I think that's a horse, not a unicorn, and riding on his back is one of King Arthur's legendary knights."

"Wow," one of the little boys said. "He's holding a shield; I can see it too!"

"Hey, you guys better take off; your folks are going to wonder where you are for so long." Kate said, as the children got up to leave. Morgan reached into his pocket but was stopped by Kate's hand on his arm. When they had gone, Kate smiled at Morgan, "You didn't need to buy them anything; they already liked you, as the man who saw King Arthur's knight on a charging steed." She paused gauging her words for a brief second, anger flashed into Morgan's eyes, changing the peaceful afternoon.

Just as suddenly, Morgan relaxed, "Sorry, I didn't mean, it's what I'm used ... to ... I wanted to make a good impression on you." He looked sheepish for a moment. "I'm not doing a very good job of this. I feel more like a teenager right now than I did when I was teenager!"

"I think it was very sweet of you," Kate began, "but we're friends ... remember? And friends don't have to impress each other. This is your chance to be the real you."

Morgan picked up a blade of grass and studies it for a moment, twirling it between his fingers. "Friends not lovers, I believe that was your choice, not mine." He said returning to the former self-assured Morgan, Kate was beginning to know well.

"Our choice, if memory serves me correctly," Kate corrected him. "I'm not anyone's lover."

"No?" Morgan raised one eyebrow in question.

"NO!" Kate replied emphatically.

"Are you afraid to be with someone, Kate?' Morgan asked.

"Only for a short time, "Kate responded, "You see," She paused searching for the right words, "I don't want a temporary lover any more than I wanted a temporary job. When I make a commitment to somebody, it'll be for keeps. I've been waiting all my life it seems for somebody to love me forever."

"So, you're holding out for marriage. Is that why you got engaged?" Morgan said, still watching the distant clouds mirrored in the blue of the water.

"I'm not engaged. That was Mike, my brother who's getting married, not me. I didn't say that very well," Kate began, "but if I were in love enough to make a commitment, I'm old fashioned enough to want marriage in my future."

Both were silent for some time when Morgan reached over and gently pulled Kate's hair, "Hey friend," He began and smiled, "how about a boat ride and then a trip through the zoo? I can't ever remember doing either with just a friend before."

Kate breathed out a sigh of relief, "I'd love to, and provided you let me help row, after all that's part of the service this restaurant offers!"

"You're on!" and Morgan pulled a happy Kate to her feet. Back on the bike again, they headed for the peer to hire their boat. The afternoon passed without incident. They took a leisurely canoe ride, bicycled through the zoo, stopped to see the Cat Country.

"Aren't they gorgeous?" Kate explained to Morgan. "St. Louis is one of the few zoos' in the world to arrange habitats very similar to their own natural surroundings for them to live in. They're not just cages. In fact, they have no bars. The high walkways above the cliffs let people watch them as if they were free." She looked sideways at Morgan, "In a way they remind me of you, the way they kind of stalk their surroundings. They look at home, as you do, but they act as if they're ready to spring at any moment to escape."

"Very astute, Kate," Morgan replied. "Sometimes, I feel like escaping from the concrete walls and endless traffic, but there's a beauty too. The Mississippi River, the arch, even this park, are all outlets for me. I guess for you too, huh?"

"Does it show?" Kate asked, "I just can't stay indoors every day for any length of time. A week, two weeks, even three but then I get edgy. I need to be able to breathe, to run." She grinned ruefully, "Not your usual sophisticate, am I?"

"No and for heaven's sake take that as a compliment!" He threw his arm carelessly around her shoulders. "You're a breath of fresh air. This may be the only time I'll tell you, but I am glad you came to R & B Inc. We may never be the same again," at which Kate nudged his ribs with her elbow, "But I am glad you came."

"Talk about a backhanded compliment!" Kate said, "But thanks all the same, I think!"

For the next hour they wondered leisurely through exhibits of penguins, snakes, and a menagerie of animals. "This huge aviary was built in 1904," Kate continued her running commentary to an interested Morgan, "As an exhibit for the Smithsonian Institution during the 1904 World's Fair. It's still one of the world's largest walkthrough bird houses and when the Olympics were held in Forest Park in the same year. It was also one of the biggest attractions, along with the invention of the ever-popular hot dog!"

"Which reminds me," Morgan took Kate's hand in a firm grip, and away from the flight cage, "I'm hungry, this time I'll treat you."

"To a hotdog with loads of ketchup, mustard and pickle relish?" Kate asked her hand tingling from Morgan's touch.

"Is there any other way?" Morgan agreed and ordered two from the outdoor vendor. "What else do we want to see?"

"Well it wouldn't be a complete trip without seeing our ancient relatives in the Monkey House, and I just love the Children's Zoo."

"The what?" Morgan questioned.

"Come on, I'll show you," this time Kate grabbed Morgan's hand and took him to the entrance of the Children's section of the zoo.

As they went through the gate, Kate and Morgan entered a nursery of zoo babies. From behind glass walls children could watch as baby monkeys were bottle fed by park rangers, and lion cubs inoculated. Any new additions were sent to the Children's Zoo for special care and observation. Rabbits, hamsters, guinea pigs and gerbils were housed at ground level and could be touched and petted. The exit from the Nursery led through a cave like tunnel into the petting enclosure, llamas, goats, and sheep followed the children over boulders and around paths much to the delight of the children. The park led across a stream bed and around a glacier like enclosure, it opened onto a tree house, a child-sized spider web, and a huge slide.

"Last one down the slide has to buy ice cream." Kate shouted as she ran laughing up the steps leading to the top. But Morgan didn't follow. He stood at the bottom and caught Kate as she slid unceremoniously into his arms.

"No fair," Kate said breathlessly from the ride but more from Morgan's nearness, his touch. "You didn't go down the slide."

"I'm too big, you're no bigger than some of these kids," he smiled, the sun causing him to squint and Kate couldn't see his eyes. He gently kissed the tip of her nose, "Thanks Kate, my friend... and now ..."

We'd better return that bicycle and head for home ... right?' Kate finished.

"Right but only on the condition we come back again," he paused, "agreed?"

"Agreed," Kate responded, happier than even she would admit to herself because Morgan had enjoyed being with her for the day.

CHAPTER 7

Kate arrived at the hospital just as Katherine Anne was being taken back to the nursery. "Oh, I missed her," she said, her disappoint showing.

"She'll be back," Leigh laughed. Motherhood seemed to give her a glow of radiance and contentment. "Thanks, Kate, for everything, Pat's been telling me all about his letter and your unexpected visit, but most of all how you got us all here safely."

Kate blushed, "Come on Leigh, I didn't do anything. I feel like a fraud with you and Pat thanking me all the time. If you insist on being grateful to anyone let it be Mary, she's the one who told us all what to do and kept an eagle eye on you at the same time!"

"I hear you,"' Leigh argued, "'but I know to whom I'm grateful. Besides, I have a favor to ask..."

"Uh-huh, get me feeling so guilty, I'll do anything for you." Kate laughed, "Go ahead, shoot, what's the big favor?"

"'Would you mind taking some pictures of Kathy? Pat and I will pay you for them, of course, please?" Leigh pleaded.

"Sorry Leigh," Kate answered briskly.

"What!?"

"You'll not pay me." Kate responded. "I have been dying to take pictures of my goddaughter all day. As a matter of fact," she paused. "I just happen to have my camera with me. I was hoping to talk you into letting me take some shots for the gallery opening."

"What gallery opening?"

"Oh, some kind of showing Max is lining up." she answered vaguely, "People just can't get enough of animals and babies. Any pictures I take, you get doubles of. I took some today at the zoo with Morgan. I'm going to include those as well. What do you say?"

"You've got to be kidding! Of course, you can use my daughter as a model. Now correct me if I'm wrong, but did you say you went to the zoo with Morgan?"

"Yes, we did," Kate responded defensively. "What's wrong with that?"

"Well nothing except that for the last month you two have been at it like two leashed tigers barely tolerant of each other, now, you casually mention you spent the entire day in Morgan's company when you didn't have to!" She paused, "Morgan is still in one piece, isn't he?"

"Leigh!" Kate tried to sound shocked, and laughed, "Morgan is perfectly fine. We just decided to put the boxing gloves away for a while, no doubt in honor of your new addition. In all confidentiality, if I didn't know any better. I'd say Morgan Buchanan was quite a guy. When he sets out to be charming... whew! ... He could set any girl into a tailspin!"

"Any girl!?"Leigh asked shrewdly, enjoying the pink that crept into Kate's cheeks.

"I also said if I didn't know any better, which I do. So ..." Kate continued strongly, "Don't start matchmaking! ...Deal?"

"I hear you," Leigh laughed, "But I for one don't believe a word of it!"

"I believe this is my cue to take pictures then," Kate responded, deftly adjusting her camera, "I'll return in a little while." She grinned as she went through the door and down the hall. As she talked with the nurses, Kate's click of her camera almost went unnoticed. As Kathy was bathed and changed, Kate took shots from countless angles, but her quiet manner didn't disrupt the nursery. As always, when Kate was taking her pictures, time slipped by quickly. It was a persistent tap on the window that finally broke into her concentration. Startled, she looked up to see an ecstatic Pat, his arms heavily laden with enough boxes to cover a Christmas tree.

"Didn't anyone ever tell you its June not December?" Kate asked slipping her camera back into her tote bag; she reached to help Pat carry his shopping spree. "Did you leave anything for anyone else to buy? Pat?" she teased as he followed her to Leigh's room.

"Delivery for Mrs. Ryan," Kate announced, "It's a store full of presents and one very proud papa." She watched self-consciously as Leigh and Pat shared a very tender moment, then excusing herself from their happy reunion she walked out of the room.

Someday I'll be in a hospital and holding my baby, Kate thought, as she rode down the elevator and someone will look at me with as much love as Pat does Leigh. She could picture in her mind the ruffled nightgown, her hair falling over her shoulders and the tiny bundle in her arms. She pictured her baby with dark curly hair. and melting brown eyes just like his father. Morgan's face floated into her dream, his eyes alight with love as he looked down on her and their baby. Morgan. Startled, Kate shook her head and proceeded out of the elevator and hospital. It doesn't mean anything Kate assured herself. It's just because you spent the day with him. But even as she rationalized why it was Morgan's face she dreamed about; Kate doubted her reasons. Oh Kate ... Kate ... she told herself, what have you done now?!

By Monday morning, Kate had almost succeeded in talking herself into believing it was just a coincidence. It was only natural to have pictured Morgan as her husband; she had seen him so frequently these past few weeks. But the disquiet remained.

Seeing Morgan standing by her desk didn't seem to help ease her mind. My, gosh, he's ... so ... masculine. Kate finished lamely, her mind refusing any suggestions. It's no wonder you thought of him, every other woman he knows thinks of him. A tiny voice echoed, and therein lies the trouble. With all those other women, why would someone like that ever settle for someone like me? You won't get involved because you don't want to risk getting any deeper than you are right now. Oh, dear, Kate thought, I know myself a little too well. Making herself appear casual, Kate walked to her desk, forcing a smile for

Morgan. "Morning Boss," she said, hoping her light flippancy would cover her confusion.

"Is it?" Morgan countered, "Get Pat on the phone right away, Kate, things are moving quickly, too quickly. Also get our file on Mike Adams-Smyth and Moreland Enterprises." He turned abruptly back to his office only to stop at his door. He ran his hand through his disheveled hair, "Kate ..." he turned to her, he started to say something when the phone rang, "Never mind it'll keep till later," and he disappeared through the adjoining door.

Kate, though puzzled by Morgan's behavior, lost no time in getting Pat and the files Morgan requested. As she took them in and placed them on his desk, she overheard his side of his phone conversation ... "its blackmail, I know it. You know it, and you can bet he knows it. I'd like to get my hands on her neck for just one minute ..." He paused, nodded at Kate as she left and continued speaking angrily into the phone.

Trouble, Kate thought, whew! I'm glad he's not that angry at me. She had sensed that Morgan would be a relentless adversary, but she hadn't been quite prepared for him in this mood. Well, better them than me, Kate thought as she proceeded to filter through the work already accumulating on her desk.

Never had the day seemed so tedious or had Kate felt so much like climbing the walls. It's time you got out of the office. Kate reasoned, back to trees and birds and clean air. No more computers and phones ringing or ...Morgan. She ended flatly to herself. Why not face up to it. You're falling for the guy just like everybody else has done or does. And you know it. One day of bliss with the guy at the park and you fall hook, line, and sinker. No, Kate reasoned. It's always been there. Ever since we first met, I've felt drawn to him kind of like a moth to a flame. I can feel his presence; his eyes seem to hold me. That's why we clashed so much. Only the clash really didn't have much to do with Morgan. It was the clash of Kate battling Kate. Maybe my sane self against any hope of ever having Morgan fall for me.

Well, it can't be for much longer. Kate reasoned, a few more weeks and the contracts would be finished. The baby's here safe and sound. I'll get a replacement; Kate thought and then leave. I'll put it behind me. I'm not going to fool myself. It'll take time, but I can and will get over ever falling for him in the first place. It's a good thing we had the sense to stay friends and not let anything else develop.

"Kate!" the intercom jolted the quiet room.

"Yes sir?" Was her carefully controlled response.

"Would you come in please?"

Kate rose, just friends, be friendly, keep a distance she muttered to herself as she crossed the area between her office and Morgan's. "Yes, Morgan?" Kate spoke as she mentally cursed herself for not calling him Mr. Buchanan.

"Pat said you like baseball. I've got some tickets for tonight's game. Would you like to go?"

Without thinking, Kate blurted out, "Against the Dodgers? That'll be a great game. Sure ..." her voice dwindled as she realized what she had just committed herself to.

"Terrific, at the rate we're working, we'll just leave from here and grab a bite to eat at the ballpark."

"Uh ... Morgan," Kate began suddenly uneasy at spending any more time than necessary in close contact with this dark compelling man, "This is just a hot dog, popcorn bite, right?..."again, she paused, "Right?"

"Well, I had thought about eating in the Press Box and don't worry about your clothes, you look fine." His head bent back to his papers, already dismissing her. Kate got up, again mentally berating herself for ever having gotten herself into this position and wondering how she could gracefully get out of it.

Quarter of six found her putting her computer cover on and clearing her desk. Morgan came through his door, looking as energetic and dynamic as he had at eight o'clock that morning. "All set?" he asked, rolling up his sleeves, revealing tanned muscular forearms.

"All set," Kate confirmed.

Kate was quiet as they left the building, conscience as never before of Morgan's hand at the small of her back, even the smell of his aftershave.

"When's the last time you went to a game?" Morgan asked as he led her to his car. But Kate was speechless as she stared at the gleaming sports car, Morgan was unlocking.

"Kate?" Morgan was enjoying her discomfiture. "Let me guess, you don't like our transportation? I think it's too far for a bike, don't you?" He smiled, showing even white teeth and a decidedly wicked gleam in the depths of his eyes.

"I had no idea ...". Kate began, she blushed at how young and gauche that sounded. She swallowed and tried again, "This is some sports car for an up and coming computer executive."

He laughed, "You're right, if computers were my only interest, they're not. Right now, they have the number one priority but once this contract is finished, we'll be rolling, and Pat should be able to take care of this operation all by himself, leaving me relatively free to take care of my other interests."

"I'm impressed," Kate said lapsing unconsciously into a friendly conversation. The tension she had felt all day seemed to disappear as she and Morgan talked on the way to the stadium.

The Press Box was a restaurant located above the stadium. A fabulous view of the field and half of St. Louis were only a few of their attractions, Kate decided as she bit into her delicious steak. "This sure beats a hot dog." Kate declared, "The food is super!"

"After the day you put in, you deserve it." Morgan said, watching with amusement as Kate ate without reservation, "Where does a little thing like you put all that food?"

"Hollow legs?" Kate grinned sheepishly, "I'm lucky I have a metabolism that burns off whatever I eat."

"It's a nice change, you have no idea how it feels to go to an exclusive club, order a dinner fit for a king and have your date pick at her food because she's watching her weight!" he added disgustedly.

"And if she didn't, you'd be the first to notice the weight she'd put on." Kate concluded shrewdly.

Morgan chuckled as he agreed she was probably right. As they rose to leave a short round man with grey thinning hair and a half-smoked cigar appeared. He gave Morgan a hearty handshake, gave Kate a wolfish whistle and sat down straddling one of the chair's they had just left.

"Your tastes are improving, Morgan... Sit down, sit down, " He said, chewing on the end of his cigar, "Thought you were going to get away without answering the question of the night ... "

Morgan laughed, "Okay, Rory, shoot, what sports trivia have you unearthed this time?"

"Who is the only pitcher in the history of baseball to have had three shut outs in a World Series?" He leaned back, confident he had stumped Morgan, but before Morgan could concede, Kate broke in, "Christy Mathewson, in the 1905 Series for the Giants."

Rory's mouth flew open and his cigar fell from his mouth, only to be caught by a shaking hand. Stubbornly he pushed the cigar back into his teeth and gritted out, "Who had the most shut outs on record?"

"In a season, Grover Cleveland, he had 16, for a career, Walter Johnson with 113." Kate shot back her eyes sparkling with mischief.

"Where'd you find her?" Rory asked conceding Kate's knowledge of the game. "She ain't just another pretty face." He stuck out his hand to Kate. "You're alright, kid."

"Thanks Rory," Kate laughed, "You're not so bad yourself." She glanced at Morgan, only to catch a glimpse of him before he caught her and spun her around in his arms.

"That," Morgan said softly, "is for being the first person to leave Rory speechless."

Kate blushed, being so close to Morgan, and having everyone in the restaurant staring and smiling at them. Morgan continued, "Rory this is Kate O'Hara, my secretary, and friend ..."He paused looking straight at Kate, "and Kate this is Rory Turner the ...."

"Radio broadcaster who telecasts live before each game with Turner's Trivia." Kate finished for him. "It's a pleasure meeting you, sir," she grinned impishly, "I've been listening to your show for a very long time."

"Fifteen years," Rory stated proudly, pleased that Kate had heard of him. "Finally, glad to see young Morgan here with a girl with spirit. Where'd you learn so much about baseball?"

"I have four older brothers who live, eat, and sleep it during the season," Kate countered, "if I wanted to get a word in edgewise, it had to be about baseball!"

"Catch my show, Kate, gotta run," He rose and gave Morgan a pat on the back, "she may be small but she's a keeper," at which he winked at Kate and was gone as quickly as he had appeared.

"Whew!" Kate breathed, "Does he always come and go so quickly?"

"He does," Morgan laughed guiding her from the restaurant and to their seats. "And, he's not used to anyone answering his questions. You threw him for quite a turn, his face was a picture. What other surprises do you have in store for me, Kate?" he asked leaning back in his box seat.

"What do you mean other?" Kate challenged, "I'm just an ordinary secretary earning her living."

"Other meaning how many languages do you speak? Remember how easily you translated for the hit and run victim? Other, meaning what do you do when you're not being a secretary? You're good but I can tell you'd go crazy working in an office every day. Other, meaning why did they call you Sister Kate at the Farmer's Market," He paused raising one eyebrow in question, "and those are just for starters."

"I thought a girl was supposed to be mysterious," Kate hedged.

"Only to capture a guy's interest," Morgan answered looking at Kate, "and we both know you don't want that; you've made that clear enough."

Kate swallowed nervously and looked down at her hands, clenched in her lap. "I'm waiting, Red," Morgan answered patiently.

76

"Four," Kate began avoiding Morgan's eyes, "German, English, of course, Spanish, and Italian and I can understand Gaelic, but I can't speak... it very well."

"One down," Morgan said encouraging her, "two to go ...”

"I help out at a home for troubled kids. I talk... with the kids it's run by Dominican Sisters to make it easier, they just kind of call me Sister Kate." Kate finished trying to make the commitment as little as possible.

"You're not telling me everything are you Kate?" Morgan asked, startling Kate into meeting his eyes. As with the first time Kate met Morgan, his gaze held hers in an almost tangible grip. Words were unnecessary, Kate felt as if he could see into her soul, read her thoughts, her heart. The first notes of the 'Star Spangled Banner' broke their hold, Morgan's hand covered Kate's as they rose for the opening of the game. He bent and whispered into Kate's ear, "Alright, little one, enough for now, I'll learn the others about you later."

His breath against her cheek, the warmth of his hand, Kate closed her eyes willing her body to remain calm. The game was a close one, the Cardinals pulling it out in the bottom of the ninth inning. Kate enjoyed herself, and she and Morgan cheered with the rest of the fans. Later on, the way home, both Kate and Morgan were quiet, something seemed to be troubling Morgan.

"Morgan," Kate began, “when I came into the office today, I couldn't help overhearing you mention being blackmailed," she paused, "Is there ... is there anything I can do to help?"

Morgan sighed, "I wish there was, but for right now, no. Thanks for offering though," He seemed preoccupied with his own thoughts, "When's the big day, Red?"

Kate was confused, "The Baptism? Next week I think, the family will all be coming home."

"Mike, too?" Morgan asked shortly. "Well of course, Mike too, he's part of the family," Kate answered, puzzled by Morgan's question.

"Of course," Morgan said into the dark of the night, his jaw tensed. His knuckles clenched the wheel, "And when is the wedding?"

"Sometime in the fall, I think," Kate continued, "Mike has to work it around his schedule at the hospital, he'll let us know in plenty of time."

"You seem awfully casual about it," Morgan said, his voice had an edge to it, "Are you sure you even love this Mike?"

"Of course, I love Mike!" Kate said her sincerity and feeling unquestionable as she strove to answer Morgan. "Whatever have I said to let you think I don't?"

"Nothing," Morgan said clipped, "Nothing at all .... He pulled into the driveway of Pat's home.

Kate was hesitant about getting out, "Thanks for the ballgame, Morgan...! I really enjoyed it ..." her voice trailed off.

"Sure," Morgan said, "We'll do it again." But even as he said the words, Kate knew they were just that, words. Something she had said had upset Morgan and Kate couldn't think what it had been.

"Goodnight," Kate shut the door and walked to the front door. Pat was still up as she went into the living room, only then hearing Morgan drive away.

"Have a good time?" Pat asked, his feet propped up on the end of the couch.

"The Cards won," Kate said, "Need I say more?"

"How was Morgan?"

"Now that's a strange question, you just saw him?" Kate remarked, watching Pat's face carefully as she lowered herself into the chair. "OK, Pat, what gives? I think it's time you told me what's going on, the blackmail? Everything."

"How'd you know about the blackmail?"

"I overheard Morgan on the phone today; I do work in the same office you know. If I knew what was going on, I might be able to help. It can't hurt can it?" Kate asked, resting her head on the chair's cushioned arm, she curled her feet up under her.

"You look about twelve years old," Pat remarked studying Kate's face, her coppery mane falling around her face and shoulders.

"Don't change the subject, Patrick," Kate said, "I'm not that easily sidetracked, not even when I was twelve years old."

Pat chuckled and sat up, "Well, it was worth a try."

"You're stalling... "

"OK, you know that we've been working to fill this big contract, well this Moreland Enterprises has a new electronic device that will enable us to decrease our computer line cost by almost a third. Big savings to us and it would give us a big edge when we put prices on the finished product. However, a big price is being asked for the device. They want, "he waited, "Morgan to form a merger, so to speak, with Moreland. The merger would be sealed by Morgan's marriage to his daughter ...”

"Marsha Adams-Smyth," Kate finished for him, "How does Morgan feel about all this?"

"He's madder than I've ever seen him! He says he won't be bought but there's a problem. We have to deliver our first shipment of the contract in three weeks, Moreland says they'll hold up delivery on some parts we need if Morgan doesn't play ball. Which means ...?"

"We can't deliver the computers, no contract, and no R & B..."

"That says it all," Pat said flatly.

"Not quite," Kate added, "I've seen this Marsha Adams-Smyth, she's a beautiful woman. Why does her father feel he has to buy her a husband? Doesn't he realize that the marriage would be doomed from the start?"

"Marsha may be beautiful but she's also very spoiled. It seems whatever she wants; she's always gotten, regardless of the cost. She's decided she wants Morgan, St. Louis's number one bachelor."

"I'll admit they've put Morgan and R & B in an intolerable situation, what about this Mike. Marsha's father, can't he be reasoned with?"

"Morgan's going to try; he meets with him tomorrow morning at Moreland, without Marsha."

"Has anyone ever gotten the better of Morgan in a business deal?" Kate inquired.

"...Not that I know of!" Pat said gravely, "You don't reach the age of thirty-five with several businesses under your power by making unwise or poor deals." He looked straight at Kate, "But there's always a first time ...Then again, having Moreland as part of his repertoire might just be worth the price, and he might just be making the better deal after all."

Both were silent after Pat's last statements. Kate felt hollow, a pain deep inside her at the thought of Morgan belonging to someone else.

CHAPTER 8

Kate arrived at work each day, feeling as if a ball and chain were hanging around her neck. Outwardly she appeared as always, calm, friendly, if one looked close they would notice the sparkle wasn't in her eyes, and the spring was missing from her step. The years Kate had spent at the orphanage covering the hurt when she was not chosen to be adopted, helped her now hide her feelings from Morgan.

She watched Morgan from half closed lids, noticing as never before things about him, storing up memories for when she would leave. The work seemed to go as usual, the same letters and correspondence had to go out, and reports had to be finished. Morgan was noncommittal about his dealings with Mr. Adams-Smyth. He spent long hours going over files, figures, and designs. He spoke to Kate as little as possible. Several times he seemed about to say something but always changed his mind. It was almost as if the peaceful interlude of Leigh's baby, the picnic, and the ballgame hadn't happened.

The sound of the intercom interrupted Kate's daydreaming. "Yes, sir..."

"Could you come in please, Miss O'Hara?"

"Right away sir," back to square one, Kate thought, sometimes I even wonder if we're friends anymore. Sighing deeply, Kate entered his office. His desk was a mass of papers and files. He was leaning back in his chair, his head resting on the cushion, his arms folded across his chest. He looked very grim; the last few days were taking their toll on Morgan as well. Lines were etched deeply across his face, his eyes seemed to be black holes, his torment tore at Kate's heart. But years of carefully schooled emotions kept her from giving herself away. "Yes, Morgan," Kate's voice softened as she tried to make things as easy as possible on him.

"Sit down, Kate," Morgan began, not missing any detail of her face or any movement of her body. She moved with the grace of a dancer, softly, without conscience thought or effort, a slight smile broke across his face, the darkness gone for a moment, "It seems more than a few days since we rowed across the lagoon or watched the ballgame at Busch Stadium, doesn't It?" At Kate's slight nod of her head, he continued, "You agreed to stay until the contracts are finished, that's in two more weeks. I'll leave it up to you to find a replacement and train her. But please" He grinned, "Let her be too old for romantic complications and young enough to train!"

Kate smiled weakly in return, "I'll see to it ... '' she swallowed, "trust me ..." her voice dwindled away.

Morgan smiled wryly, "Trust me she says. Believe it or not Kate, I think I could learn to trust you." There was silence, each filled with their own thoughts.

Kate rose nervously from the chair, "I won't let you down, Morgan, I promise." She turned toward the door, only to stop when Morgan began speaking again.

"Sunday's the Baptism for out goddaughter. I know things have been rather strained between us. I'd like very much if somehow, we could go back in time, for Leigh and Pat and be ...friends... again for them. I don't want anything to spoil their day." He paused. Kate could almost feel his eyes searching her mind, willing her to turn around. But she fought against his magnetism.

"I'd like that. Morgan...even though things seem to have changed, I still thought of myself as your friend ... "Inwardly, she thought it'll take more than this to stop my heart.

"Thanks, Kate. I'll see you on Sunday... Is the whole family still coming?"

"Everybody and anybody that's ever known or heard of Patrick Jonathon Ryan are coming!" She turned, the smile covering her face causing her eyes to light up. When she was happy, Kate's face turned from pretty to very lovely, and Morgan watched never more aware of a woman's beauty that radiated from within. "Have you ever met the entire Ryan clan?" at his shake of the head. "You'll never forget it. I know I won't ..."She stopped realizing her lapse. She hurried on hoping Morgan wouldn't be aware of it. "How come you never had the privilege of meeting the family? Didn't you and Pat spend four years at college together? I know Ma and Da wouldn't have let him alone that long!"

"No." Morgan agreed. "But you know your family. Money was tight. Pat used to hitchhike home on holidays. I never saw them on campus except for when we graduated. I remember meeting a small blonde woman, not unlike yourself, who literally moved everyone out of her way so that she could watch her son accept his diploma. He received more letters in a month than I received ..." He stopped," I guess all of you were writing to him from home, I think he had a girlfriend, too".... Kate looked up startled, "He used to get some from Southern Missouri, somewhere in the Ozarks. He used to read and reread those letters. I don't know what happened to her, he just said they were from someone special." He hesitated, "When I contacted him about this job, he didn't hesitate. I guess it just didn't work out ...I sure would like to meet her though."

Kate smiled a secret smile, oh Morgan, you have, you have.

"Maybe you will Sunday," Kate added.

Morgan laughed, "Maybe, but at least I'll have a few friends there amongst all those relatives."

"We'll be your safe port in a storm, right?!"

"Something like that," Morgan added. "Why don't you go on home? It's getting late, there's nothing that won't wait till later."

"Alright," Kate added surprised, "and thanks, there are a lot of things I need to do to help Mary with, including Kathy! See you Sunday," Kate walked out the door, closing it softly behind her. Her smile disappeared as she gathered her things and quickly left, praying that Morgan wouldn't change his mind and come through the door and question the tears, Kate couldn't keep from running down her cheeks.

Sunday dawned into a beautiful early summer morning. The air was fresh, clean, crisp, birds sang. Leigh's garden was overflowing with a myriad of colors; vines clung to the patio archway, as climbing roses created contrast against the white fence bordering the walkways. Kate stood on the wet of the dew-covered grass, reveling in the beauty all around her. She was still in her nightgown, a thin housecoat wrapped carelessly around her waist, her hair still a mass of disarrayed curls. She leaned against the trunk of a towering oak. She breathed deeply, there's something about the early morning air, and Kate thought that seems to cleanse the soul. Nothing seems so hopeless in the bright sunshine. Worries seem to multiply in the dark of night but looking out at the sun rising slowly over the horizon makes the problems seem to dwindle, almost diminish in size. Another day, a christening of a new life, surely only happiness could be expected on a day like today.

The slight crack of a twig alerted Kate of her coming intruder. She turned her head, smiling at Danny as he walked towards her, carefully carrying his cup of coffee. He still looked more asleep than awake, Kate mused, dressed only in hastily clad jeans. His hair gleamed in the sunshine. "Good morning," Kate broke the silence of the moment.

"It will be after I drink this cup of morning elixir." He smiled ruefully, "How can you manage to appear so wide awake so early in the morning?"

"I can't stand to miss the best part of each day. I never tire of watching the sun rise, or of watching as the entire world comes alive, "she laughed, "even you!"

"Minx!" Dan teased; he put his cup down and sat on the ground, looking out over the house tops, trying to see the morning as Kate did. "Do you miss your woods and trees Kate?"

"You know I do," she cried out, then bit her lip, "I've enjoyed being here with Pat and Leigh, but things are back to normal, or as normal as they'll ever be again with a new baby around. My time is ending. I expect Max to call any day now, berating me my extended vacation and piling on heaps of assignments that have come in ..."

"Which you'll take with joy," Dan added, "because you'll be doing the work you like best in the places you like best and besides," He said slowly, "it'll keep you so busy you won't have time to think about one Morgan Buchanan."

Kate raised shocked, hurt eyes to look at Dan's understanding ones, "What ... what do you mean?"

"If you're worried that everybody knows you're in love with the guy, relax. Pat and Leigh only see Kathy, Mike's all tied up with Katrina, and Sean has decided he likes this nurse you have hanging around here. I wouldn't be surprised if we had two engagements announced. Then there's me ... "He reached out to gently touch her cheek." From the first time I met this boss of yours. I could sense trouble; you forget I was there when you clashed at the dinner club that night. You could almost touch the sparks flying between you two. Then I saw your face when he appeared unexpectedly at the house a while back. I've also been watching your carefully controlled mask that you don every time his name is mentioned which is pretty often. A mask means you're hiding something, my guess, you've gone and done something like falling in love..."

"You should have been a private detective instead of a teacher." Kate laughed shakily.

"Sometimes they're the same thing," Dan said, "I know he's not married so what's the problem?" he waited, then spoke angrily, "if he's hurt you in some way... "

"You mean if my honor is in jeopardy?" Kate smiled sadly, "No, Dan, nothing so Victorian." She took a deep breath, "it's not very complicated, really. Morgan and I became friends, nothing mysterious, by accident we happened to spend some time together; I made the mistake of falling for him, which he doesn't know about, thank God! Anyway," she pushed her hair back from her face, "A business partner has put in a bid for Morgan's ... services ... so to speak. If Morgan marries his daughter, he'll give him a device that'll save R&B millions. If he doesn't comply with his wishes, he'll ruin and bankrupt the company by delaying a shipment that's due."

"Who's the lady in question?"

"You met her, in fact, remember the blonde at the dinner club, that's her Marsha Adams-Smyth."

"Whew!" Dan whistled, "Certainly not a fate worse than death to be married to that for life ... uh sorry Kate but she was a looker!"

"I know," Kate agreed, "I really don't see Morgan disagreeing. I think he'd agree except for the fact that it's not his choice or inclination.... she paused, "He has a bit of a ... playboy... reputation and I've a feeling marriage is not a priority in his life nor in the near future." Kate concluded wryly. She glanced at Danny, "and none of your non-fail plans that never failed to get us into trouble. This is my problem and I'll handle it myself!"

"You can't handle it by going back to your negatives and running commentaries on the life and times of the American Squirrel?" Dan spoke roughly, "Don't do it Kate, you can't hide forever from feeling. You took a chance at the Ryan clan, was that a mistake? Don't run away from love ..."

"Even if it's one sided?" Kate cried. "Don't get me wrong, I know Morgan could want me, there's a physical attraction but for how long, Dan...A week, or a month, a year? I want someone for life, someone to love me forever. Is that too much to ask?"

"Love doesn't come with a written guarantee. When you fall in love you have to take a chance," He ran his hand through his hair, searching for the right words to say. "Would you trade the times you've spent with Morgan for twice as much time away from him?"

"Of course not," Kate assured him..." But ..."

"...But nothing." Dan said, "you know for the last twenty years, you've never spoken about your parents ... I know it hurts ... For reasons unknown to us, your mother was forced to leave you in a home. Maybe she was dying, maybe she couldn't support you, maybe just maybe instead of wanting to get rid of you, she loved you enough to give you up, because that way she felt you had a chance at growing up with two loving caring parents." He took Kate by the shoulders and gently shook her, "Let the past go, Kate, live and love with your whole heart, don't be afraid because of what you think happened to your parents!"

Tears ran down Kate's face, Kate who never cried, but seemed to have cried more in the last few weeks since she came here than in her whole life. Her arms went around Dan, her head resting against his chest, "Oh, Dan, what am I to do?"

"It's all right to cry it out, it'll be okay," Dan assured her. But his forehead was creased in thought, wondering if there were any way that he could help her.

Kate stood beside Morgan in the front of the old cathedral, holding a doll sized bundle. Kathy's long white dress trailed far beyond her toes, and even the tiny bonnet covering her hair seemed too large. The church was filled with relatives watching the elderly priest baptize her. As Morgan gently removed the bonnet, Kathy's hair caught the sun; the small wisps seemed to reflect their light. Kathy seemed unaware that anything special was occurring as she contentedly sucked her thumb throughout the entire ceremony.

Kate was filled with a wonder at the tiny infant in her arms, gently cradling her against her heart. To Morgan, she looked the perfect Madonna and Child. His breath seemed to catch in his chest, she was so perfect, so natural holding the baby in her arms. Thoughts of wanting her to hold his child came unbidden, unwanted to his mind. Thoughts that try as he might to ignore, they proceeded to fill his waking moments and disturb his sleep as well.

As Kate looked up, catching Morgan watching her, she smiled a smile for him that came from her heart. It took Morgan a considerable amount of self-control not to take her in his arms then and there.

The words of the priest as he sprinkled the holy water broke into their moment, and Kathy's cries of outrage at the unexpected wash, quickly made them turn to her once more. The ceremony over, Kathy was sadly relinquished back to her proud parents. As they walked from the church, countless relatives stopped them to admire their newfound joy.

Kate knew that Morgan was behind her, without looking she could feel his presence, knew it was his hand at her elbow. Her skin tingled from his touch, her mind a confused jumble of her feelings and Dan's words repeating themselves over and over.

She glanced up nervously at Morgan, "They kind of take your breath away, don't they?" hoping to ease the strain of so many unknown people.

"Someone does," Morgan spoke softly back. He watched as her cheeks filled with color, and chuckled, "Alright, Kate, tell me who all these people are, provided you know of course!"

"I sense a challenge of some sort in those words; just remember after I introduce the third Aunt Anne and the fifth Uncle Daniel that those are family names and repeated generation after generation."

"I hear you," Morgan conceded, gently tucking Kate's arm firmly in his, "With this many people, I'll agree you probably ran out of names and had to use them over and over again."

"How about we start with Pat's brothers?" Kate inquired.

"You're the tour guide; you can start with whoever you want." He paused, "Believe it or not right now they all look the same, except for the few who have your red hair. Does it run in your family?"

"It's a throwback to ancient relatives." Kate explained, "And tends to show up unexpectedly in each generation. For example, Ma was a blonde and Da was the typical black Irish rogue, but they had Dan ..."

" .. And you," Morgan interrupted.

"... Who received the ancient curse of red hair?"

"Not a curse, Kate ..."Morgan corrected, "Think of it as a glowing crown only a few are privileged to inherit."

"I'll remember that the next time you refer to me as 'Red'," Kate said shakily.

"Touché'," he said graciously meeting the people who stood between them and her brothers. She felt Morgan's hand tighten as they approached for some reason; she had never felt Morgan would feel nervous meeting Pat's family. The thought that even Morgan might be vulnerable made her feel protective. She smiled inwardly at the thought of her being able to protect this six foot plus giant. Kind of like the parable of the lion and the mouse, Kate mused, weaving them towards Dan. Dan watched as they came closer, Kate seemed to glow, her arm tucked protectively in Morgan's large presence. He noticed the softening of Morgan's face as he spoke to Kate, the gentle teasing that flowed between them. His mind was plotting, if that could be the right term, he grinned as they approached, Kate, old girl, Dan thought, I just might have a solution, at least it'll give you a chance.

"Now that was a nice feat of maneuvering Kate," Dan said as she arrived with Morgan. He put out his hand, "I believe we've met, at the country club."

"I remember," Morgan said politely, "I don't believe I caught the name."

"That is our baby brother," Sean interrupted, as he and Mary arrived.

"... and you're the elder brother with the arrested development," Dan said sadly and in an undertone to Morgan, "He still plays with boats in the bathtub."

As everyone laughed, including Sean, Mike arrived a radiant young woman on his arm, "Break it up you guys. You're creating a scene! Do I always have to be the referee between you?" Mike laughed.

"This," Dan said seriously to Morgan," ...is our younger elder brother, alas, he still plays doctor. I doubt there's much hope for him. He's even thinking of keeping a nurse with him day and ... night," He added wickedly.

Kate shook her head, loving them even as she saw how confused Morgan seemed to be. "Wait a minute! Time out guys!"

she broke in between the bantering. "Morgan this is my family. Pat you know he's the oldest, then there's Sean," she pointed to the naval officer," and Mary, she was the heroine of saving Kathy and Leigh, our own private nurse. "Then she poked Mike in the ribs, "This is Mike. Soon to be Doctor and Mrs. Ryan," she winked at Morgan, "He's set the date for August, and I'll never know why, but Kat's agreed," she paused," and last but not least this is Dan." She looked again at Morgan, "This you clowns is my boss, Morgan Buchanan, so be nice, you don't want to get me fired, do you?"

They broke into a confusion of voices, as they all started talking to Morgan at once. Morgan looked blankly from one brother to the next, but his gaze kept returning to Mike and the young woman on his arm.

"That's Katrina Evans," Dan said in an undertone, "she's marrying Mike," he watched as that information sunk in, "You heard about it that night at the house..."

"I...I thought she said that Mike and Kate ... Kate was kissing him ...Kat not Kate," he spoke almost to himself, but Dan heard and as he heard, a grin spread over his face. Better and better, he thought.

"Listen," Dan interrupted the group, "I think it's time we headed for the house to the reception. What do you say?" Dan wasn't leaving things to chance, "Kate why don't you go ahead with Sean and Mary, you two seem to be running the show."

"I'll take Kate with me," Morgan said firmly, "there's a few things I need to know."

"Later," Dan said taking charge quickly, "I'll ride with you, Morgan, keep you company; you'd be amazed at the things I could tell you about Kate."

His eyes met Morgan's for a clash of wills, for once Morgan conceded, his slight nod of the head let Kate know that he was allowing Dan to win. What's Dan up to she wondered and threw a warning glance at him as she left with the others. Dan's angelic shrug of his shoulders did little to quiet her fears.

As they watched her walk away, Dan turned to Morgan, "After you," he said politely.

"My car is this way," Morgan said, as he took long strides down the church steps to the parking lot.

Dan whistled as he caught sight of Morgan's car, "What a beauty!" Tongue in check, he added, "too bad you're thinking about selling it.''

"But I'm not," Morgan returned briskly.

"I must be mistaken then, I heard you were about to be married. This isn't really a good car for a wife and of course children."

Morgan's jaw tightened and his eyes seemed to flash. Both men got into the car. "Perhaps you'll tell me who divulged that bit of information to you, Mr. Ryan?" his voice was a silky as steel.

Dan looked out the window, "I don't recall, actually," He said, carefully planning his next words.

"I could convince you to remember," Morgan said menacingly.

"You could," Dan said, a smile on his lips as he watched Morgan, "but then I wouldn't tell you how to get out of this 'mock' marriage and still save R&B. The decision's yours of course."

"Of course," Morgan repeated. Silence prevailed for some seconds when Morgan continued, "You know, Mr. Ryan, I don't know why but I like you, I can't imagine a solution we haven't thought of but then, what have I got to lose?"

Dan laughed, "It's the red hair, Morgan, you think anyone with hair the color of Kate's can't be all bad."

"Don't push your luck, Dan." Morgan warned, "Now what's this miracle solution. In three days', time, I have to spend an extended weekend with them in their cozy cabin."

"Perfect!" Dan cried, "It couldn't be working out better!" As they drove through the suburb leading to Pat's house, Dan outlined his plan. Morgan listened, asking questions occasionally.

As they pulled into Pat's driveway, Morgan turned to Dan, "Your plan just might work, provided all the characters involved agree. But tell me why this interest in my forced marriage?"

"Well" Dan hesitated, "I'm a bachelor, too, feel we're a vanishing breed, just wanted to help out one of Kate's old friends."

"So, I'm not going to get a straight answer on that one?" Morgan concluded, "If this goes as planned, will you tell me then?"

"If this goes as planned, I'll tell you," Dan agreed.

"Right, who's first on the plot line?"

"Pat and Leigh, Never talk to Kate unless you have a stacked deck. Against the four of us, she doesn't stand a chance."

"I sense you've been up against Kate before?" Morgan queried.

"You have no idea!" Dan exaggerated, and then paused, "I do think the timing is important, too, we'll catch Pat and Leigh after everyone is gone, then Kate. She'll be exhausted after all this and ...”

"... she won't feel up to fighting us all off?" Morgan finished.

"You're catching on," Dan grinned. "Those were my thoughts exactly. Ah Kate ... Here we are at your service." He mocked as Kate greeted them at the door of the garden.

She eyed Danny suspiciously, "Daniel Kevin Ryan, you're up to something, I can see it in your eyes."

"Kate," Dan said, his blue eyes twinkling, "You mortally wound me. I hope the food is ready, we're starved."

"Daniel," Kate began, only to be stopped by Morgan's arm on her shoulder.

As she turned her head in question, Morgan asked, "Is there anything that needs to be done?"

Kate watched the laughter in his eyes and the look that passed between them; she threw up her hands and exclaimed, "You're in this together!"

Morgan answered amusement twitching his lips, "In what together, Kate?"

"Kate!" Mary called.

"Coming!"' she said and then threw a warning glance at Morgan and Dan, "You two are up to something... "

"Rubbish," Dan declared kissing her on the cheek, and then added innocently, "Mary's calling."

"Dan," Kate tried again, this time it was Morgan who kissed her cheek, his breath warm on her face. Kate blushed, her hand going up to touch her cheek.

"Scoot, Red," he said softly, "We'll tell you all later... I promise." In confusion, Kate turned to shake a warning finger at Dan and then disappeared into the kitchen.

"She knows you well," Morgan said to Dan.

"Too well," Dan said ruefully. "Now I ask you do I look that guilty."

"Like a cat that just swallowed the canary."

"Oh well," Dan said good-humoredly, "Que sera, sera! Come on, I'll introduce you to our relatives ... just don't question my knowledge when I introduce you to three Aunt Anne's..."

"... and four Uncle Daniel's, they're family names," Morgan finished," I also know that the red hair is a, to quote Kate, a curse that crops up."

"Myself, I like to think of the hair as our link to the infamous Finn McCumhail. You have heard of Finn? "

"No," Morgan grinned, "But I have a feeling I'm about to!"

"Yes, well ..."Dan continued. He kept up a running dialogue for the rest of the afternoon with Morgan.

Meeting all the relatives, getting to know Kate's brothers, for the first time in his life Morgan felt a part of a family. He watched Kate as she moved from group to group. She was clearly adored by all, Dan watched as well, liking Morgan the more he talked to him. Yes, Dan, he patted himself on the back; you've really done it this time.

"Daniel Kevin Ryan," Kate shouted, "You've really gone and done it this time. You've finally gone one hundred percent certifiably insane!" she looked accusingly at the complacent figure in the living room chair. Dan didn't seem upset in the least; she ran a hand through her hair pushing back the heavy strands. Then turned to stare at Pat and Leigh, who instead of agreeing with her, were in firm agreement that Dan's plan just might work. Then there was Morgan, Kate avoided looking at him altogether, Oh, what must he be thinking! Kate cried inwardly, Dan, I'll murder you for this, Kate promised herself, shooting silent daggers at Dan's back. She turned back to the foursome, "Let me just see if I've got your plan correctly, Daniel!" Kate said sarcastically, he winced. "If Morgan tells Mike Adams-Smyth that he's in love with someone else, namely me, and that his marriage is doomed from the start. You think he'll give in and deliver the parts and put a monetary price tag on the electronic device, getting Morgan off the hook and R&B Enterprises."

"You've got it," Dan grinned. "It's so simple it just can't fail!"

"In the first place, who is going to believe that Morgan Buchanan, rich, playboy and St. Louis's number one bachelor is going to trade it all in on his lowly secretary?"

"But Kate, through working with you each day he's come to love you!" Dan answered patiently.

"In the second place, who's going to believe he'd choose me over the lovely glamorous Marsha?" Kate countered. "Tell me Dan, would you?"

"Geez Kate!" Dan said. "You're my sister. What kind of a question is that? I wouldn't go so far as to say you're glamorous, but you have a definite appeal!"

Kate shook her head in exasperation when Morgan broke the silence. "Rory Turner."

"What?" Kate asked.

"Rory Turner would believe I'd choose you over Marsha," he explained.

"Rory Turner is only one person in the entire city... "Kate cried out.

"...who millions of people listen to and particularly Mike Adams-Smyth. Rory is his brother-in-law." Morgan added, "And a large share holder in Moreland."

Silence fell upon the room.

Kate walked to the window, her mind a battleground of indecision. She leaned tiredly against the pane, the coolness of the glass momentarily easing her tension. Dusk was falling, fireflies and crickets began their flights and nightly rituals. Kate sighed, and then tensed as she felt Morgan's presence behind her.

"Do you remember asking if there were anything you could do to help Kate?" Morgan asked, his image reflected in the glass.

"Yes," Kate murmured turning to look up at him with troubled eyes, "and I'd do it except for two very important reasons. The first is that nobody will believe you're ... the least little bit in love with me instead of Marsha ..."

"Trust me, little one," Morgan spoke softly, reaching up to run his finger down her nose and to cup her chin, "I'll be very convincing. I think it would surprise you, Kate, to know how other people see you. Marsha's beautiful, I won't argue with that, but it' s only on the surface. I can't imagine her stopping to help an accident on the street or leaving a job to help her family or" he grinned, "managing to meet my requirements in a secretary. You do all of those and more. People look for more than beauty in choosing a mate," he waited for her to continue.

Kate swallowed nervously, touching dry lips with her tongue. Her hands twisted before her. "I... we ... I... don't think I could ... would it be a very good idea .... She blushed, "Would there be a lot of kissing?" she blurted out, avoiding Morgan's eyes.

"Do you find it so distasteful to kiss me?" he asked, his voice very low so that only Kate could hear. The others seemed to disappear.

So that Kate was only conscience of themselves "...Morgan ..." Kate said hesitantly, "you know that's not the case at all, I think you're very much aware of the opposite, which is the problem. We decided on friendship, that means a lot to me ... I'm afraid of what might happen ...to pose as your fiancé. We'll be together a lot..." her voice trailed away.

Morgan put his hands into his pockets and looked first at Kate and then outside to stare moodily at the growing darkness. Kate wished herself anywhere but here beside Morgan, and yet so far away... she wished she could read his thoughts, to know what he was feeling.

"You once asked me to trust you, remember?" Morgan began, "Now I'm asking the same of you, trust me Kate, I promise I won't let you get hurt or ... in over your head. Will you do that, Red?"

"If memory serves me, you said that was asking a lot ..." Kate laughed shakily.

"Ah ..."Morgan smiled, "but you're better at trusting than I am."

"You think so?" Kate smiled wryly, "I'm as crazy as the rest of you are, alright, Morgan, I'll trust you." She turned large green eyes towards him and put out her small slim hand, "Friends?"

"Friends..." Morgan said, decisively enclosing her hand into his large one. Mentally promising himself what he'd do if anyone were to hurt her because of him. Together they turned back to the silent trio on the couch.

"Well, Pat and Dan," Kate said, "Aren't you going to congratulate your newly engaged sister?"

"You're going to do it!?" Dan cried jumping to his feet, "Not that here was ever any doubt, of course," He smiled.

"Of course," Kate grinned.

"Now, there are some plans to be made if this is to work... "Morgan said, taking charge of the situation. Kate silently crossed her fingers; making a wish that she was doing the right thing.

CHAPTER 9

"Why do I have to have a ring?" Kate asked stubbornly. "It's a big waste of money. I can just as easily wear Ma's."

"For the umpteenth time, Kate..." Morgan said patiently, as they parked outside the jewelry store. "It's a beautiful ring and heirloom, but not the type people are going to expect me to give to the girl I marry." He paused and squeezed Kate's hand, "I want to buy you something for going to all this trouble for me."

Kate was silent staring out the window, "I don't want you to buy anything for me because I'm helping you." She looked at Morgan, "...friends don't buy gifts, they just say thanks and return the favor someday."

"Oh no ..."Morgan cried, "I hope we never have to go through this again!"

"Point taken," Kate agreed trying very hard not to smile, "It's just I know how expensive rings are... "

Morgan broke in, "and I can afford it! ... Now will you please smile, and act like you're happy and pick out a ring!"

"All right," Kate surrendered, "I'll pick out a ring."

"And if you pick out the first one you see just to get it over with Kate O'Hara ... I'll turn you over my knee," Morgan threatened.

"YOU wouldn't dare!" Kate shot back.

"Try me," Morgan said quietly. He got out and came around to Kate's door. "Is this going to be our first pre-marital disagreement, Kate?"

"Probably," she said, as she got out, "But not our last."

He chuckled, tucking her hand into his arm, "That I can well believe, "Which brought a smile to Kate's face, making them appear the happy newly engaged pair they were posing as.

"Mr. Buchanan..." the storekeeper said, "Come right this way, Mr. Browning is waiting for you in his office."

Kate whispered to Morgan, "He knows you by name; you must be a regular visitor." She looked around her at the very plush, exquisite surroundings.

She noticed Morgan's slight smile, as if pleased by an inner thought, about to ask him, they reached the executive offices.

"Mr. Buchanan," Mr. Browning extended his hand nervously. "If you'll be seated, we have the rings you requested on the tray over here ..."

On the black velvet cloth laid a dozen of the most breathtaking diamonds Kate had ever seen. Sensing her refusal, Morgan motioned for Mr. Browning to leave. Seating Kate himself, he took her hand, "Okay, Red, which one do you like?"

"You can't do this," Kate whispered, shocked, "Don't touch them, until he comes back in the room. He might think we're trying to steal them." She looked nervously around annoyed when Morgan laughed.

"No, he won't I promise." he took her hand again, "Trust me, Kate, now which one?"

"How much do they cost?" Kate asked, her timidity quickly being replaced by curiosity. "I've never seen anything like them before ... are they really real?"

"You're not supposed to know the cost!" Morgan laughed. "and yes, they're definite, genuine real diamonds. Now can we get on with this?" He watched her face, trying to see which one she gazed at more, trying to judge which would be her choice.

But Kate only grinned and stuck out her hand, "Surprise me!" she said impishly, before she closed her eyes.

Morgan surveyed the tray, expertly judging their merits on Kate's hand. In his mind there was no question. He placed an emerald, surrounded like a small flower with diamonds on her finger. Kate opened one eye, then the other. Looking at the delicate craftsmanship, her eyes were alight with her approval of Morgan's choice.

"It's beautiful. Morgan ..." Kate said softly. "Thank you ..."

Morgan leaned forward and gently brushed his lips against Kate's, "That's the way engaged couples thank each other," he reminded her, "and you're very welcome." He smiled. "It really couldn't be any other ring to suit you, emeralds to match your eyes and the shape of a blossom opening."

Kate looked down at the ring to hide her thought, oh Morgan, she cried inwardly. If only you were saying those things for real. She was saved from having to answer Morgan, by the return of Mr. Browning.

"Did you find one to suit your needs, sir?" He asked.

"Yes, Browning, we did," Morgan answered, grinning as Kate blushed, "You may be the first to congratulate us on our formal engagement."

"Engagement, sir... "Browning asked, "We were led to believe ... My heartiest wishes, sir, on your forthcoming marriage. When is to be the lucky day?"

"Soon" Morgan answered pulling Kate to her feet and putting a proprietarily arm around her shoulders, drawing her to him ... Kate's blush deepened, Morgan was enjoying her discomfort, "Very soon," He said bending to kiss her firmly before ushering her out the door.

"Morgan!" Kate said mutinously between smiling lips, "You enjoyed that!"

"I sure did," He agreed, helping her into the car. "Now back to the office, and I'll wait for Mike's call. You see, Red, Mr. Browning is a very close friend of his."

"Oh," Kate said, understanding why Morgan had been as he was.

"Have you found a replacement yet?" Morgan asked, deftly switching the subject to neutral ground.

"Yes, I think I have," Kate explained, relieved. "She's been with the company for a few years but only as a clerk, however, Mrs. Ross has been taking night classes in order to qualify for a better paying position. One, she's someone we know and trust, two she's happily married with three children, teenagers, I believe, and third, she has much better qualifications than anyone working for you has ever had. I think you'll find her a goldmine!" Kate concluded.

"Sounds perfect, "Morgan agreed, "But time will tell if she works out that way... You'll be a hard act to follow," he added.

"Just give her a chance," Kate pleaded, pleased at Morgan's comment. "Now what's next on the agenda?"

"...Office wise or being engaged?"

"Morgan ..." Kate began.

" ... I'm sure the newly efficient Mrs. Ross can handle the office; we are going to do what all newly engaged people do, after Mike calls of course, spend the day alone!"

"Aren't we getting just a little carried away, let's just go back to work as usual, ok?" Kate tried.

"If people are going to believe this is for real, we need to do all the things we're supposed to do, right?" Morgan reasoned pulling up in the R&B parking lot.

"Right," Kate agreed, secretly looking forward to a day with Morgan. "So, where so we go? What do we do? I've never been engaged before!"

"Me either," Morgan said wryly, "We'll decide where after Mike calls. See if you can pick out a place without phones."

"Aye, Aye, sir," Kate said as they rode the private elevator to the executive floor. "I'll start Mrs. Ross with the work on the desk," Kate assured him, as Morgan nodded and went into his office.

Kate held her breath when the phone rang only minutes later, the caller unidentified but authoritive in demanding Morgan Buchanan.

Kate pushed the intercom, "Morgan... Call on line three ...I think...it's the one you've been ...expecting." She was very conscience of Mrs. Ross sitting beside her.

As Morgan spoke Kate could hear the determination in his voice, "Put him on, we have a lot to discuss, don't we Kate?"

"Yes," Kate answered quietly, "Good luck, Morgan... "She whispered as she transferred the call, her heart and thoughts with Morgan as he talked to Mr. Adams-Smyth. Kate had trouble keeping her mind on Mrs. Ross and the training at hand. Questions were repeated several times, as her concentration kept straying towards the closed door. When Morgan opened the door sometime later, Kate jumped, her gaze riveted to his face, searching for some sign as to the success or failure of Dan's plan. But Morgan gave no outward sign of the result of his talk with Moreland Int.

"Ready?" he questioned, looking very grave and unapproachable in his tailor made suit. Kate saw Mrs. Ross stare in awe as he approached the desk. Oh, no thought Kate, not another casualty to his good looks. She nodded, inwardly wondering how to deal with the problem of any romantic ideas developing.

"I'll meet you by reception in five minutes," Morgan said, looking at his watch, then broke into a smile at Kate's expression, "I need to catch Pat for a moment."

"Perfect," Kate said, carefully planning her words of warning for Mrs. Ross. As he left, Kate turned towards her, "Susan ..." she began hesitantly.

"He sure is a fine specimen of a man, Miss O'Hara," Mrs. Ross interrupted, "He sort of took my breath away. If I weren't so happy with my William, I just might be charmed into falling for that young man." She spoke in a rush, while calmly putting the paper into the teletype. "Not that you'd ever have anything to worry about, Miss, he has a special look for you. I've worked in the office here for several years, I've seen a good many attempt for his affections. He's been quite the man about town, but never," she paused and smiled at Kate, "Have I seen him look at a woman like he does you."

Kate was relieved, embarrassed and pleased simultaneously while she listened to Susan Ross prattle on. She blushed, gathering up her purse as she hurried to join Morgan, thinking about what Susan has just said. Silly woman, Kate thought, but at least she's competent and she doesn't have any designs on Morgan which is a relief. Wondering against her will if he did have a special look just for her, probably one of exasperation Kate decided as she hurried from the elevator to meet an impatient Morgan.

As he opened the door for her, she looked up at him surprised to find him watching her, a smile on his lips, his eyes twinkling as he watched her try and keep up with his long strides. "You know, Red, I always forget how small you are!" He laughed at her immediate indignation.

"There's nothing wrong with my size, Morgan Buchanan!" Kate began defensively.

"Calm down, Kate," Morgan soothed, "I never said there was anything wrong with your size, as a matter of fact, I'd say you packed a lot of woman into a pint-sized body!"

"Yes ... well," Kate stammered, "When you say it like that, I don't know if it's good or bad!"

"Good, Kate." Morgan grinned, "Very good. That was definitely a compliment."

"Then thank you," Kate said, and then added, "I think."

"Should I ask where we're headed?" Morgan asked.

"Nowhere," Kate announced firmly, as they approached Morgan's car. "You can take me home."

"Now Kate," Morgan began, "You can't be upset about the remark about your size ..."

"Mr. Buchanan!" Kate said, interrupting him, by turning and pointing a finger at his chest, "I have patiently waited to hear what is going on but you ... you act as if nothing is going on!"

"Ah ..." Morgan said, smiling, "I wondered what could have set you off this time, not that I haven't seen you get angry before of course."

"Morgan!" Kate cried, "Please!"

"Well now that you've asked so nicely, "He said as he shut the car door and began the engine. Morgan was as expert at driving as he was at other thing, in and out of the heavy downtown traffic, Morgan maneuvered the car.

Finally, Kate could stand it no longer, "Morgan either you tell me here and now what's going on ... or ... I will get out and walk!"

"That's a pity," Morgan said, not intimidated in the least, glancing sideways to notice Kate's flushed cheeks and rapid rise and fall of her breasts as she sat. "However, since we are in this together..."

"Morgan..." Kate warned. "I am trying very unsuccessfully to be patient, but you are not helping at all. Would you just tell me!"

"Alright, Red," Morgan replied, grinning, "By the way did anyone ever tell you you're beautiful when you're angry?"

"NO!" Kate cried, throwing up her hands in frustration, "They've never lived so long!" she muttered darkly beneath her breath.

"I'm duly frightened," he chuckled, "Alright, yes that was Mike on the phone; Browning lost no time in phoning him. To put it in a nutshell, he thinks it's a fake, a cover."

"I told you!" Kate cried, "I said nobody would believe you'd choose me over ..."

"Kate, shut up!" Morgan said firmly, "That's not what I said. Mike doesn't believe it about anybody. He hasn't seen you or us together; let's just say he's skeptical."

"What?" Kate asked perplexed.

"Mike doesn't believe any of it, he's just realizing I'm not going to be that easy. He's invited us down for the week to his getaway cottage. He wants to see for himself how serious we are."

"Oh, no," Kate began, "I'm sorry Morgan; I guess that kind of puts an end to it. There's just no way... "

"We're going." Morgan announced with finality.

"We're what?!" Kate repeated, "We can't! We couldn't! Have you gone crazy, Morgan?"

"No." Morgan said firmly, he pulled into the parking lot of a restaurant. His arm went to rest against the back of Kate's seat, he turned to look at Kate. "Look, Red, you said you'd help. What's the difference of pretending here in St. Louis and going and doing the same thing in a different place?"

"But Morgan..."

"If this is what it takes to convince him." He sighed, watching Kate carefully, "You know I never thought of you as a quitter. Kate. We've only just begun and already you're ready to bailout."

"I'm not a quitter," Kate stuck out her chin stubbornly, missing the laughter lurking in Morgan's eyes, "I ... it's just that circumstances are changing--I, wasn't ... I'm still not prepared for any of this." She stopped and looked out the window, anywhere but at Morgan, "I don't want to let you down or back out, but Morgan I don't think I can pretend all day, every day. I'm not very good at keeping secrets. You said so yourself at the ballgame, remember?"

"I said," He stressed, "You were full of surprises and contradictions. I'd say you've done a good job at keeping secrets about yourself, aren't you, little one?"

Kate kept staring ahead, her mind a confused jumble."Just try it," Morgan urged, "It's out in the country, you like being outside instead of cooped up in an office. We're newly engaged, they'll expect us to spend a lot of time by ourselves, that'll save a lot of questions from the others. Does that sound too difficult?"

"Do you ever not get your way, Morgan?" Kate asked quietly.

"A few times," He answered, watching the sun catch her hair, "I remember how a certain young lady became my 'temporary' secretary against my wishes."

"... and see what's happened because of it!" Kate said sadly. She looked down at her hands, clenched in her lap. "What do we have to do?" she asked, finally daring to look up at his dark form.

"That's my girl!" he said, and then proceeded to kiss her soundly. He touched her lips with his finger, grinning roguishly.

"What was that all about?" Kate asked her body still tingling from his touch.

"Call it practice." He said as he watched her quivering lips, "You know what they say..."

"No," Kate smiled shakily, "What do they say?" trying to match his teasing manner.

"That practice makes perfect." his eyes glinted dangerously, as his hands tightened on her arms, drawing her closer.

"I think they're perfect as they are," Kate said quickly.

"Oh?" Morgan asked, "That's nice to know ..."

"That's not what I mean," Kate added, already trembling from Morgan's overwhelming nearness. "You're not playing fair" She whispered.

"I know," He said softly before kissing her lips once more. Then gently he pushed her back into her seat, his hand touched her lips lingering in a caress and then he released her. "I promise to play fair, in love and war." He teased easing the situation.

Kate smiled her senses still clamoring for his touch. "Maybe..." she said as ran her tongue over her lips, "...we should discuss this over lunch?"

Morgan smiled, and nodded, "I think, little one, that would be a very good idea."

Kate was quiet and subdued. Lunch was ordered and eaten in silence. Morgan was patient, choosing to let Kate reconcile in her mind her indecision. As their meal drew to a close, Morgan spoke, watching Kate closely for her reaction, "You know, Kate, how is it you've never asked me about my parents or my past?" he waited.

Kate was startled and completely unprepared for dodging his questions; she stared at Morgan for long seconds before looking down at her hands. She took a deep breath before answering, "Usually when you ask about someone's family or past, they do the same."

"And you don't like answering questions about yourself, do you Kate?"

"I just like my privacy, that's all" Kate answered lamely, biting her lower lip nervously.

"Do you think it'll come up in the conversation this week at the cabin?" Morgan asked, "For instance, they'll wonder how your parents reacted to the news, or mine? Do we get along with each other's families? How do we answer, Kate?"

"As truthfully as possible," Kate replied her voice little more than a whisper. He knows, she thought, he knows about me. But how? From who?

"That's what I thought," Morgan agreed, "That's why I think you should come home with me tonight and meet my family. Seeing as how yours know all about this, it might come as a shock to mine, possible hearing it from strangers."

"Oh, no!" Kate cried, panic already rising in her heart, "I can't Morgan, please don't ask me!"

"Let's go," Morgan said, leaving the money on the table and steering Kate out the door and to the car in silence. Kate sat numbly watching trees pass unnoticed, uncaring of her destination, rehearsing in her mind how to tell Morgan about her past. He won't want to go on with this masquerade, Kate reasoned, that would be a relief. But Kate felt no relief at the loss. It will be the shortest engagement in history, she mused, staring at the sparkling ring on her hand. She blinked back tears, fighting for composure.

It took some minutes for Kate to realize Morgan had stopped the car. He sat patiently waiting, watching the row boats circle the quiet lagoon.

"Why are we here?" Kate asked, the lump rising in her throat making it difficult to talk.

"You said you come here to think, I'm hoping to talk too. I don't want you hurt; I want to know what I'm doing to make such a panic appear in your eyes. Are you terrified of me?" She shook her head, "Then what is it? Can't I help?" He leaned back against the seat, his arms folded across his chest, his long legs stretching before him.

Kate swallowed convulsively, "I'm not the sort of girl you should take home to your parents ..." She began to tell Morgan all about her past and how she grew up. By the waters of the lagoon as she talked, not daring to look at him for fear of the revulsion she'd see. "I'm not really Pat's sister. I mean I am ... but I'm not. I was left at the orphanage when I was born. I met the Ryan's when I was six. I feel like they're my real family, I love them like they were. I wasn't legally adopted until I was eighteen. I learned to speak other languages because of the Sisters at the home. They were from different countries. Sister Suzanne was German, Sister Mary Therese was Spanish, and Mother Dominica was Italian. Father Hannigan was Irish, he taught me Gaelic. Not all at once, but when you're around people for eighteen years you learn. English was our universal language." Kate continued, almost as if Morgan wasn't there. "I found out early that there isn't a big demand for red haired orphans. But I was happy, you see I had the Ryan's, every summer, I belonged. It didn't seem to be that important anymore. You grow up the same as everybody else. I learned from dating that I was considered inferior. I wasn't as good as everybody else, to their friends, I was second best. I finally had one of my dates lay it on the line for me. I was fine to date, but I wasn't the kind to marry, who knows what kind of children we'd have or history I held." Tears flowed down her face unheeded. "After all if my own parents didn't want me, who else ever would?" Her chin trembled and then stopped as she added, "I'm not ashamed of my life, but I ... I'll understand if we just forget the ...engagement and the weekend ... and everything." Only then did she dare to glance at Morgan. He, too, sat staring out at the softly running waters, his jaw was tightly clenched, and his body was tense. "Morgan ... I'm sorry... I know you're angry, I tried to tell you at the house when this all came up, but I..." Her voice trailed off.

He turned his head to look at Kate, his eyes blazing "Angry! Of course, I'm angry, I'm furious and I'd love to get my hands on that date of yours for just five minutes, he'd never have the nerve," He gave a sarcastic laugh, "or the teeth to be so cruel again." He reached over and took one of Kate's hands, holding it firmly but gently, his thumb moving slowly, caressing over her skin. "I'm not angry with you, little one." His voice lost some of its gruffness. "But I am at a lot of other people, my own family for instance." He paused to wipe the last of Kate's tears from her cheeks with his handkerchief. "You know Kate. I almost envy you." She looked at him in shock at his words, "You see your parents gave you up, mine didn't. I spent my life growing up at boarding schools, except for the occasional card or gift at Christmas. Summers I was shuttled to my Grandparents or summer camp. I don't remember ever feeling at home even at home. I overheard my mother talking to her friends one day, how she hated the very sight of me. I reminded her every time she saw me of her lover. She said she could almost see his sneer when she told him she was carrying his child. I learned to sneer, partly to add torment to my mother and partly because it was the way I felt. My father, the man who paid the bills at least wasn't unkind to me. I often wondered if he knew about my mother's affairs. He died several years ago, leaving me as his heir. I couldn't take his money. That's one reason I decided to make my own and not just use or live on his. Maybe I'm really my father's son after all. Ironic if my mother had been wrong, all these years. I was unwanted too, and my parents told me every time they didn't write or phone how much I meant to them." He was silent then, still holding Kate's hand, her answering squeeze made him look at her, her wobbly smile lighting her eyes.

"We sure are a gruesome twosome, "she said, "A couple of unwanted misfits."

Morgan matched her smile, admiring her spirit, "I guess we're more alike than we knew, sort of made for each other. We can tell them a match made in heaven!"

"Let's not go that far..." Kate rolled her eyes, and then grew more serious, "I'm sorry Morgan for bringing up unpleasant memories, I just didn't want to cause you any... embarrassment."

"Never," Morgan said positively. "And that I know I can trust will never happen." He started the car, "Now," He raised his voice ominously, "Let's go meet the wicked Witch of the West."

"Are you sure? Kate began, "Not because of what I am," she smiled, "But because it will only be for a short time?"

"No, one thing my mother never could keep was a secret. I'll tell her when it's all over." Morgan said, so firmly, Kate knew better than to argue.

"Yes, Morgan," she agreed meekly, happy to know Morgan still liked her regardless of her past. Maybe he could even learn to love me, Kate dreamed, then sighed, content just to be his friend and be with him.

CHAPTER 10

"Oh, Leigh..." Kate cried, throwing her hands in the air, "I give up, I'll never in a million years get all these clothes in that suitcase!"

Leigh sat on the bed grinning at the confusion around her. "Are you leaving any clothes behind? Maybe we should be concerned, you and Morgan could be planning an elopement?"

"Even that," Kate said wryly, "Might be easier than a week with Ms. Adams-Smyth."

"Oh?" Leigh raised questioning brows "I've been meaning to ask you about that ..."

"About what..." Kate responded, searching through her drawer for the belt to her suit.

"About your loving Morgan," Leigh said, intently watching the blush rise in Kate's cheeks and how her hands nervously folded the lingerie on her dresser.

"Don't ... don't let your imagination run away with you ... this," she held out her hand, her emerald sparkling, "is all pretend, remember?"

"Oh, I remember," Leigh said, surer of her hunch, "I remember how you avoid talking about him, how you glow after you've been with him. I remember how I was about Pat; I seem to recall it all very vividly. It was fantastic and frightening because I was afraid, he didn't return my love." She paused, "are you worried that Morgan doesn't love you?"

"No," Kate answered firmly, flatly, "I know he doesn't." She turned to stare at Leigh, "sorry, to ruin your dreams that it will all work out. But Morgan as you told me that first night is not the marrying kind. I ... we're just friends."

"You know, I could believe you until I see you with him," Leigh smiled reaching out to touch Kate's arm, "Either you're head over heels in love with Morgan or you should win an Emmy for your performance. It's not something you should be ashamed of ..."

"Not ashamed," Kate said sitting down heavily, "and yes," she smiled at Leigh, "I love Morgan... just like all the rest of his legion of broken hearts ... but to Morgan I'm just a friend."

"Have you told him?"

"No!" Kate said quickly, "He'd bolt like a rabbit, I won't embarrass him by confessing I love him, I'll just store up all these memories, when we part ... as ...friends, I'll pull them out one by one, " she said sadly, then smiled, "Someone famous once said 'it's better to have loved and lost than never to have loved at all, '" she straightened up, "Now, I'd better get a move on or one of those memories will be of Morgan when he throws all these clothes into the suitcase himself because I'm not ready!"

"I'll agree patience is not one of his virtues," Leigh said, "but then I've never known Morgan to be so dense either!"

"He just thinks I'm acting," Kate replied, "Now, how about if we sort through these clothes one more time. Are you sure I'll need an evening gown? This is a cabin in the country isn't it?"

"Oh, Kate..." Leigh cried, "Your idea of what a cabin is and there's are nothing alike. Trust me; you will definitely be dressing for dinner. The jeans and swimsuit are fine but you're competing with the fashion plate of the season so ..."

"Be prepared...right?"

"Right..." Leigh cried, then rising, "I think I hear Kathy, let me check and I'll be right back. I still want to hear about Morgan's mother ... "She left the room as Kathy began to cry; her tiny wail stronger as she heard Leigh coming.

Kate smiled ruefully, she wants to hear about Morgan's mother, the Mrs. Buchanan, and according to her, and the only one there will ever be. Mrs. Buchanan was beautiful, her hair in a very carefully done coiffure, the silk dressing gown elegantly showing her a very youthful looking woman. Her eyes, Kate remembered most vividly, grey-cold eyes. Carefully assessing her but choosing to ignore her presence as she spoke.

"Hello, Morgan," she had said," and what brings you here today?"

"Hello, mother," Morgan said emphasizing the word mother as they walked further into the room, his arm guiding yet held protectively around Kate. "This is Katherine O'Hara."

"Not your usual sort of woman is she Morgan?" Sylvia Buchanan muttered beneath her breath, meant for only Morgan to hear but Kate did as well.

As Morgan stiffened, Kate smiled, slipping her arm through his, "I'll take that as a compliment, Mrs. Buchanan, I've met some of his 'women'."

"I see," Sylvia replied thoughtfully, "and where does that leave you? Or should I say what exactly are you to my son?"

"She's my fiancée," Morgan spoke distinctly, watching his mother's carefully controlled mask slip.

"But you can't!" Sylvia cried, "Not to her!"

"I can and I will," Morgan's voice was firm.

"But why?!" she asked, forgetting or choosing to ignore Kate's presence in the room entirely, "Of all the suitable women in the world, why her? Sleep with her if you must but not marriage for God's sake!"

Morgan's whole presence radiated anger at his mother; Kate quietly slipped her hand through his arm, and squeezed gently. Letting him know she understood. He looked down at the small fragile hand resting on his arm. He smiled; slow warmth spreading to his eyes as he noticed her concern, amused that so small a person could hold such strength.

Kate turned to Mrs. Buchanan, "What a lovely home ..." she said, hoping for a safe topic.

"Are you pregnant?" Sylvia asked flatly, ignoring the warning signals from her son, choosing to set her aim on the small figure by his side.

Kate's eyes flashed, "Whether or not I am pregnant is none of your business. The only business that should concern you is the happiness of your son."

"Ah ..."Sylvia smiled wryly, "The kitten has claws. I should have guessed as much. My son would not have settled for anything else. My son," she laughed tonelessly, while dismissing his presence with a sneer," has been a disappointment to me, to you, too, I'm sure Miss O' Hara once you're around him all the time."

"I think not," Kate said quietly, her Irish temper and contempt for the situation overriding her good intentions to remain on the sidelines. "The disappointment you see is not in your son, Mrs. Buchanan, but in yourself and the life you've chosen, not him. How anyone could have anything but respect and admiration for Morgan and all he's done. He's quite a man, one any woman should be proud of as her son or her husband." She dared not look at Morgan, but stared stonily at his mother and said, "I think it best we leave, Morgan, it seems we've caught your mother at a bad time. We'll come back later."

"... Or not at all!" Sylvia shouted, "Heed my voice, Miss, there's only one Mrs. Buchanan and there will never be another one—ONE, do you hear me!!"

Morgan and Kate left quickly. Kate was surprised at the many feelings surging in on her...pity...anger...understanding of Morgan's bitter trust of women. Silence stretched uncomfortably while they drove home, but somehow not home as they arrived back to the lagoon. Kate leaned back in the comfortable Mercedes, watching the graceful swans, geese, and ducks effortlessly moving across the water in Forest Park. She sighed; aching for the hurt and pain Morgan had grown up with what he was feeling now.

"There's a saying the sisters used to tell us at the orphanage," she began softly; searching for words to ease his wounds, "what we are is our gift from God, what we make of ourselves is our gift to God." she paused.

"Kate's words of wisdom..." He queried one large hand reaching over to cover her two small ones. The growing dusk sending his features into shadow, it was difficult for Kate to read his thoughts.

She nodded, wordlessly, "I ... I'm sorry about the scene ..." He began...

Kate hushed his voice with her finger, "It's not necessary, I do understand." She smiled, teasingly, "It was exciting, though, you sure know how to show a girl a good time!"

Morgan chortled, and then laughed a deep rumbling sound deep from his chest. He gathered Kate into his arms and squeezed till she felt her ribs would crack. "Oh, Kate!" Morgan whispered, and she thought she heard him add 'My, Kate.''

"Kate!!" Leigh shouted again, "Your errant knight is here!"

"Is he wearing his frog suit?" Kate shouted back, grinning as she descended down the stairs carrying her suitcase

.

"Watch it, Red," Morgan grinned devilishly, "You better be nice to me, you have to spend a week with me, ALONE, in the middle of nowhere. This is not the time to make wisecracks."

"I'm truly chastised and will act accordingly," she said meekly before she playfully poked Morgan, tickling his side as she handed him her suitcase. "My life rests in your hands" she batted long lashes at him.

"Hold that thought!" He laughed, as he took her suitcase surveying her trim shapely clad jeans, plaid shirt and denim vest .

Kate blushed as he finished his observations, "Well, do I pass muster? You did say casual, didn't you?" Her eyes traveled over Morgan's faded jeans and the leather vest he wore exposing a dark hair covered chest, his muscular legs plainly showing through the worn material. Kate swallowed at his sensuous masculinity, her voice only a whisper, "I can change ..."

"I hope not!" Morgan said solemnly, "I like you ..." He paused searching her face and gently placing a kiss on the tip of her nose "...in that outfit. It fits quite nicely..." He grinned, watching Kate blush. "Come on Red," he continued going down the stairs, "We've a long way to go. Bye Leigh, wish us luck!" and he was through the door before either Leigh or Kate could get another word in. They looked at each other, eyes wide with surprise and promptly burst out laughing.

Leigh hugged Kate to her, "I'll wish you luck, I can see you're going to need it."

Kate crossed her fingers, "Let's hope it's a short week, right?" already wondering if it was too late to change her mind. A returning Morgan ushered her into his car before she could back out. She gave a great sigh while he walked around the car to get in, glad of an entire week with Morgan, regardless of the circumstances. One more week to store up my memories, she mused.

Hours later still found them travelling across the many miles of Missouri and Illinois farmland. "It always amazes me," Kate said gazing at the growing crops, "How much we take for granted."

"Do mean people or things?" Morgan asked, one eyebrow raised, his strong hand handling the powerful car with ease.

"Both," she returned, "Look at these fields, each one plowed, fertilized and planted, in the fall, harvested. We go and pick up whatever we want at the store, pay for it, eat it, all without giving a second thought to the hard work that goes into each product. Even before, of the bit by bit of land clearing the pioneers did, taking the untouched land covered with waist high prairie grass and slowly painstakingly claiming the rich soil as farmland."

"Very philosophical," Morgan countered, "What brought such thoughts?"

Kate grinned, "I received a letter from Dan. Did he tell you about the Ryan roots?" At his shake of the head, "He will, it's his hobby. History is his passion. For instance, did you know that the first Ryan's came to America in 1652? As indentured servants, no less, all the way from Galway County in Ireland. Nimrod Ryan worked as a shipbuilder up in Massachusetts. He worked off his service and married his boss's daughter. Inherited the business as his father-in-law died and promptly brought over the rest of his relatives. Dan just found a deed from Andrew Jackson giving some land to the Ryan's for helping with the war of 1812. Here to Illinois, they traveled lock, stock and barrel. The diary he's reading was from one of the first Daniel Ryan's. From the work described, Dan's very glad he decided to teach and not farm!!"

"From the sound of it, so am I!" Morgan agreed heartily, "Keep your eyes open for a place to eat, all this talk of crops has made me realize how hungry I am!"

"Me, too!" Kate countered, "That billboard just advertised for some pizza, how does that sound?"

"What kind?"

"Garbage... What else!" Kate laughed.

"... and what," asked a puzzled Morgan, "pray tell is a garbage pizza?"

"It's got everything but the kitchen sink on it, with lots of mozzarella cheese!" she licked her lips, "They are so...o...o good!"

"Sold!" Morgan grinned, "A garbage pizza it is!"

"I'm stuffed," Kate groaned, as they settled once again into the car, "I don't think I'll be able to move again." She paused, "How much farther is it?"

"A couple of hours," He grinned, "Why don't you take a nap. I'll wake you before we get there," at Kate's questioning glance, "I'm sure, I'll be perfectly fine driving, besides I want you bright eyed and looking beautiful when we arrive."

Kate closed her eyes, "Morgan," she murmured.

"Yes, little one?" answered an indulgent Morgan.

"What did you do after college?"

"I thought you were going to sleep?"

"I am, I mean I will," Kate assured him, "I've just been wondering that's all. There's a big gap between college and when you and Pat joined forces. I know you made it on your own," she paused, curling up her legs under her, resting her head against the seat, "I'm not prying, just curious. If you'd rather not tell me, I understand ..."

"It's not a secret," Morgan said watching the road winding before him. "I took a job in Texas, settled working for the other company and then my own. My friend ... helped ... he was retired, but just wanted to stay busy. We were starting to make it ... financially, when I was drafted, two years during the most important time. George came out of retirement then and agreed to oversee the business. I left; we were still struggling. I poured my soul into the company along with my pay from the service. A similar company was in trouble, I took a chance and bought in too, with two companies, we bought bulk and saved. But the gamble paid off--Electronics products soared and we flourished. We added more and more floundering companies, then George ... died," Morgan paused.

Kate touched his arm. "I'm sorry," she whispered, her voice husky with compassion.

"So am I," Morgan continued. "He was family to me." Silence hung heavy in the car. "I met Pat again, a year or two later. We talked about what we'd been doing; we combined our ideas, my money and designs, his expertise and connections and decided to form our own company. The rest you know ... "

Kate smiled, "Thanks, Morgan."

His hand came over and covered both of Kate's. "Think nothing of it, Red, " Morgan teased, back to himself.

"Alright then," Kate quipped, "I won't. Goodnight, Morgan," and Kate closed her eyes, her deep even breathing soon telling Morgan she was asleep.

It seemed only minutes later that Morgan was gently shaking her shoulder. As she drowsily opened her eyes, Morgan kissed her lightly, making Kate's eyes open wide, sleep the farthest thing from her mind.

"What was that for?" she asked. A bemused Morgan kissed her again, smiling as he raised reluctant lips.

"I believe that is the correct way to awaken a sleeping beauty. Is it not?"

"Are you Prince Charming?" Kate questioned, silently wanting his lips to descend once more.

"Touché'" Morgan said ruefully, "Although to be honest, I have been told I am charming and also called a prince ...of a sort." He paused smiling, "Never in the same breath though."

Pulling her thoughts together, Kate looked around her, realizing that while she slept, Morgan had left the flat farmland of central Illinois and driven deep into the Shawnee National Forest. Morgan had pulled off the road, atop one of the many mountains. As far as one could see were thick, lush green topped trees, the slight musty smell of leaves lying dormant under the brush. Birds circled in the evening's dusk. Kate took a deep breath an overwhelming feeling of coming home.

This is where I belong, Kate thought. Life is less complicated, much simpler. She turned to look at Morgan, "How much farther?"

"About five minutes, they're the only cottage for quite some way." He paused, "Ready, Red?"

Kate smoothed her hair, and straightened in her seat, she nervously twisted her ring, somehow gaining strength from the tiny band of metal circling her finger. "Ready," Kate answered firmly, "Or as ready as I'll ever be!" she added.

"That's my girl," Morgan said, and gently touched Kate's chin with his fist, "and in case I forget, thanks."

Kate's laugh was shaky, "Better wait till it's over, heaven only knows what this week might bring!"

Morgan was silent, a gentle shake of his head to refute Kate's statement his eyes never leaving Kate's face.

CHAPTER 11

Thank you, Leigh! Kate thought as they turned into the winding lane leading to the cottage on the hill. Cottage! Now that's a laugh, who would ever call this 16-room mansion a cottage? The outside blended in well with its surroundings the rough cedar exterior, the overhanging balcony, even the swimming pool was cleverly designed to look like a small lagoon nestled beneath the towering oaks. Tennis courts could be seen to the left as well as a heliport.

"How quaint," Kate murmured, "All the comforts of home ..."

Morgan's deep chuckle was heard before he answered. "... and then some!!"

"I'm wondering who thought up the term cottage. I would think mansion...or... estate... or even a hotel would be a more appropriate description." She turned to Morgan. "Have you been here before? Did you know all about this?"

"In answer to your questions, no ... and yes ..." He opened the car door. "I've heard rumors of their get away, but it didn't prepare me for all this."

"Having second thoughts?" Kate questioned playfully. "Just think all this could be yours if you pick bachelorette number #1 ..."

"Yes, but since I have to take contestant #1 as well... forget it!" he laughed. "What comes with bachelorette number #2?"

"Yes, well nothing so grand. I'm sure. Let's see, an enormous family, a shrew for a wife, to quote your term, and absolutely no strings attached," She paused. "Well, what do you think... have I got a chance?" She fluttered her lashes more serious than Morgan knew.

"You'll win hands down." He helped Kate from the car, kissing her soundly as he pulled her from the car into his arms. Kate's arms circled his neck before she could resist. His hands holding her close, she felt the entire length of him, reveling in his touch.

The sound of a door slammed, and Morgan slowly raised his head, her knees felt weak, Kate felt glad of his support. "Ready for Act One, scene One, little one?" he said softly, still raining feather light kisses on her eyes and then the tip of her nose.

"Do we have retakes?" Kate asked her hands gently pushing against his chest.

"You're on dangerous ground, Kate," Morgan growled, his eyes sparkling with mischief.

"How's that saying go?" Kate said grinning, "Once more with feeling...?"

"Any more feeling, Miss O'Hara," He said into her ear, " ... and this will be no imaginary engagement. Understand?!"

Kate blushed, "Yes, sir... "She said, tossing her suitcase to him, and managing to evade his reach for her at the same time.

"Good evening," a cold voice behind them said, they turned to find a glamorously dressed Marsha standing there. Her blonde hair falling loosely about her shoulders, the black crepe dress clung to her, the slit up one side showing long slender legs as she advanced closer.

"Good evening, Marsha," Morgan said turning back to pick up the suitcases, he grinned at Kate as he did, "You've met my fiancé before ..."

"Ah ... yes," Marsha drawled, "the temporary... receptionist."

"Secretary," Kate corrected firmly, meeting the distinct challenge she was receiving from the other woman. Speaking carefully, "This is a beautiful ... cottage, Miss Adams-Smyth."

Morgan stepped in promptly, "If you'll show us where to put our things ..." and he walked up the driveway, ushering a reluctant Kate before him, leaving a very angry Marsha to follow.

Marsha showed them to a luxurious suite. She explained that they would have to stay together, because all the other rooms were being remodeled. It was an inconvenience, but necessary all the same. She left the two at the door and told them she'd meet them for dinner shortly.

Kate's voice was low but there was no mistaking her fury as she faced a determined Morgan in their room. Eyes flashing, Kate exploded, "Do you honestly believe that in this entire mausoleum this is the only room available, that the others" She mimicked, "are being redecorated ...and since we're engaged ... tee, hee ... they thought we'd prefer this ... this ... setup?"

"Set up is right, Kate," Morgan rubbed a hand absent mindedly across his forehead, mentally berating himself forever having considered coming to the cottage in the first place"...We don't have a choice, Kate ... You make a fuss about another room and Mike will know something is not right."

"Are you going to tell me ... ALL engaged couples sleep together?" Kate asked, her arms folded before her, crossing and re-crossing the room ..."Well?"

"It has its possibilities... "He began, only to be interrupted by an exploding Kate.

"The only possibility is for us to pack it in if this whole thing is hinged on whether or not I sleep here ... tonight with you ... then the whole game is over."

"Alright Kate, let's look at it another way, let's say we do get you moved to another room, without upsetting the engagement. What's to stop Marsha from paying me a visit later on?"

"You're a big boy," Kate bit out angrily, "You'll think of something... "

"Not looking down the end of a gun ... for a shot-gun wedding for compromising his daughter beneath his roof ... No matter how innocent I am ... "He paused, "We keep the room arrangements the way they are... "

"We darn well won't," Kate began again, "I am not going to sleep with you!"

"I didn't ask you to, at least not here ... " He crossed the room to confront Kate, "This is a big room, from outside appearances we'll be sharing this room, this bed. I'll sleep on the couch over there. You can be safe here ... trust me, Kate." He paused to touch her shoulder, "I said you'd be safe with me ..."

"I know ... I do trust you Morgan, " Kate said, raising anguished eyes to him, it's me Kate thought, how can we stay here together so close and still not let you see how I feel ... it's such an explosive situation.

"Then we stay...?" Morgan raised one eyebrow, questioning.

"We stay," Kate said, woodenly.

"That's my girl" Morgan smiled, swinging Kate around off the ground. As he steadied her back on her feet, "I'll not compromise your virtue, Miss O'Hara," He teased," but now we need to get ready for dinner ..."

"Tux and tails, just a simple little meal," she mimicked Marsha again, "Lobster, fresh from Maine, and caviar from Siberia ... nothing fancy, you understand ... just plain down-home food ... "

"Minx," Morgan laughed, "Do you want a shower first or second?"

"First," Kate decided taking a robe from her case and walking to the adjoining bathroom, "I'll need all the time I can get to meet Marsha on her own turf... I have a feeling this is a no hold barred fight! ... Besides" She flicked a towel at Morgan, "Ladies before gentlemen" and she disappeared behind the door.

Sitting on the side of the bathtub, Kate turned on the taps. A deep sigh and tears crept slowly down her cheeks. Oh, Morgan, how am I going to be so near you and yet forever hide how I feel ... shaking her head and drawing a hand across her eyes to dry her tears? I may look the poor fool to Morgan, but Marsha is in for a fight. Put me in the same room as Morgan, will you? He doesn't deserve that witch. She slipped out of her clothes and into the steaming water. Tonight, Kate thought, I'll go for an Oscar.

Slipping into the cream-colored gown, Kate again thanked Leigh for packing for every contingency. She twisted to zip the back of the dress. Her back was to the door, she did not see Morgan enter.

He walked silently to her side, "Allow me," he said causing Kate to jump nervously at his nearness.

"Thank... thank you." she murmured as he finished zipping her dress.

"You see," He smiled, showing even white teeth, "Having me in the same room could be an advantage. No telling what I could be doing for you."

Ruefully Kate grinned, "I'll bet you could, but sorry... I'm an independent type. I like to do things for myself. Now, you could try Marsha ... "she let the sentence trail off.

Morgan winced, "Claws back in Kate, remember we still want the Moreland Contract, just not the merger." He tipped Kate's head back and kissed her forehead, "You, Miss O'Hara, look beautiful. You remind me of my Greek history, classic lines, your titian hair, body men would go to war for and eyes that even a siren would envy..."

Kate looked into the mirror of the dresser; her hair was swept up, leaving a few tendrils, her gown reminiscent of Roman togas. One shoulder was held by a gold clasp, the empire waistline falling smoothly, hinting at the curves beneath. Morgan looked devastating in his black tuxedo, his shoulders looking even broader beneath the smooth material. His hair was still damp from the shower. Kate took a deep breath, "You don't look so bad yourself..."

"Watch it," he grinned, "I might take that for a compliment. It wouldn't do if we actually said something nice to each other for a change?"

"Don't act so surprised," Kate responded saucily, "I was nice to you the entire way down here ..."

"You slept!!" Morgan grunted.

" .. But wasn't I nice to you to sleep most of the way down?" Kate doggedly continued." It could have been worse. I could have talked about the weather, fashion, or ... work the entire trip!"

"Point taken," Morgan raised both arms in surrender, "Now are we ready to go down and face our opponents?"

"Ready," Kate said taking his arm, "willing, and " she paused impishly, "itching for a fight!" At which they both left the room, laughing.

As they walked down the hall to the stairs, Kate was struck again by the simple lines throughout the entire house. Arched doorways, dark wood contrasted against cream colored walls and thick plush carpets that cushioned your every move. A Cathedral ceiling showing open beams made the living room the center of activity. French doors opened onto a virtual paradise of flowers and ferns. A constant battle with the ever-creeping nearby forest, as it tried to reclaim its once virgin ground.

Voices were heard, and they followed them, knowing they belonged to Marsha and her family. They were drawn to yet another room, one directly off the living room. As they entered, Kate gasped instantly aware of the interest in her hosts as all eyes turned towards their entrance. It was all Kate could do not to show her revulsion at the display of Mr. Adams-Smyth's trophies. The walls were adorned with the heads of Mr. Adams-Smyth's hunting prowess. Morgan's hand came up to gently squeeze her own at once giving her strength and comfort. He understood.

"Morgan!" A hearty voice boomed from across the room.

"Mike, this is," and Morgan softened his voice, "My fiancée, Kate O'Hara."

"Mr. Adams-Smyth ... " Kate said, offering her hand to this big burly giant, for he was taller even than Morgan, the years had thickened his chest and waist, years of outdoor living giving his face a ruddy, weathering, "your home is beautiful but I'd be less than honest, if I didn't admit to my astonishment of this room ..."

A great guffaw of laughter seemed to come from deep within his chest, "Call me Mike, Kate. So ..." he proceeded to direct them to a large leather sofa, "You don't like my game room?"

Kate met him squarely, "I've always found killing for sport a cruel and wasted activity. I prefer to see these animals alive, in their natural habitat ... and" she added, "If they need to be shot, I prefer it done with a camera."

The glass eyes of the mounted heads seemed to stare down at the gathering, bear, deer, elk, geese lined the paneled walls, Kate shivered, conscience of Morgan's hand tightening around her own, as if to lend his support.

"So, you don't approve of Daddy's hobby?" Marsha added.

"It's not up to me to either approve or disapprove," Kate tactfully added, "I merely stated I prefer live animals to the heads of dead ones."

" .. And you Morgan," Marsha asked sweetly, touching his arm, "how do you feel about all this?"

Kate swallowed; the entire trip could be ruined because of her tactless statement. She looked down at her hands not daring to glance at Morgan, fear of the anger she might encounter.

"I've lived in the city most of my life ..." Morgan began as if searching for the correct words, "there's not been much chance to watch animals on their own. I've always been fascinated by their ability to adapt to changing times ... " he paused, "but like most hunters, I've always found the chase--exciting" he slid his arm around Kate, pulling her toward him, "the captured prey intoxicating, I'm afraid I agree with Kate, I would prefer a warm body as opposed to just another trophy to hang on the wall."

Kate gazed up at Morgan, shocked, thrilled at his analogy. Her eyes glowed as she understood Morgan's comparison to hunting and his bachelor days. The warm dark compelling eyes of Morgan's held her.

"Surely a match made in heaven," Marsha drawled sarcastically, she too, catching the hidden meaning.

"To each his own," Mike agreed, secretly admiring their stand against him,

"Weren't you in the service Morgan?" he asked as he handed a glass of wine to each of them.

"Yes," Morgan said slowly, "I can't say that my experience didn't help sway my feelings. I understand a man killing for self-defense, I can understand killing for self-preservation, for food, but to kill simply to show superiority over nature strikes me as an unfair advantage. Guns have always given man the upper hand; I prefer gaining the upper hand by my own cunning."

"Understood," Mike agreed readily, "Now how about some dinner?" He held out his arm for Kate, "If you'll allow me?" Kate had little choice but to take his arm and follow him into the dining room, leaving Morgan to escort Marsha.

The dining room was yet another beautiful combination of subtle colors and hues, the crystal-clear glasses reflecting the pristine whiteness of the tablecloth against the flicker of candlelight. Places were set for six; Kate raised questioning eyes to Morgan as they sat down. Marsha smiled, like a cat who swallowed a canary, Kate guessed shrewdly bracing herself against whatever lay ahead. Pretending concern at the inquiring glance at the empty places, Marsha murmured, "We do have a few other friends here as well." She paused, "Perhaps you've met them," her eyes glittered dangerously, "my aunt, Wanda Turner ... " she raised questioning brows first at Kate and then Morgan.

"Rory's wife I presume?" Morgan said politely.

" .. And" Marsha added looking directly at Kate, "a very distant cousin of mine, Craig Warner," dropping her bomb squarely into Kate's lap.

Afterwards Kate was very thankful for the mask she was able to wear for the rest of the evening. "Craig...?" Kate smiled, "I haven't seen him in years. How nice ..."

Confusion drew Marsha's brows together, unprepared for Kate's controlled reaction. "Yes," she went on, "we happened to be talking the other day, your name just popped into the conversation. He mentioned knowing you," she dropped her voice insinuatingly, "quite well as a matter of fact, I believe intimately was his choice of words."

Kate smiled meeting Marsha eye to eye, "I'm sure it would be."

Morgan sitting across the table, watched the by play between the two women aware of the tension curious as to who this Craig was and what role he had played in Kate's life.

"I assume they'll be joining us for dinner?" Kate asked politely.

"Yes," Mike countered, "Craig hadn't seen the stables we recently added, and Wanda said she'd do the honors."

"You have horses, too?" Kate asked.

"Yes, about time, too," Mike said, "I love good horse flesh, a good brisk ride in the morning, nothing could be better for waking a person, getting the cobwebs out." His broad smile showing his pleasure, "Do you ride Kate?"

"No," Kate shook her head, "I love animals, though, I'd love to see them while we're here."

"What a pity," Marsha said, "Morgan is such a good rider. I'd hate to see him miss out simply because his fiancé doesn't ride." She paused lowering her eyes, "Perhaps you'd allow him to ride with us in the mornings?"

Much to Marsha's surprise, Kate laughed, "You surprise me, Marsha! I thought knowing Morgan as you do that, you'd know what I 'allow' or not wouldn't make much difference. Morgan's his own man, single, engaged, or married!"

Morgan grinned, his eyes meeting Kate's, "You know me well, love!" He said amused at Marsha's tactics, and at Kate's answers. "I think I'll pass, if you don't mind, Mike, I want to spend as much time with Kate as possible ..."

Marsha's response was lost as Mrs. Turner and Craig entered through the French Doors. "So sorry to keep you waiting," a lovely woman said, speaking to the room in general. She was about fifty with dark brown hair liberally sprinkled with grey. Her round face and bright blue eyes fit well with the slightly plump figure. She looked about the room with interest, finding Kate quickly, "You have no idea how much I've wanted to meet you, very few people can out stump my Rory, He's still talking about you." she smiled holding out her hand to Morgan, "Rory said you'd pick a winner..."

"So, did he," Morgan said rising gallantly taking the hand before him gently between his own.

Wanda blushed, "You'll have your hands full," she said in a very loud whisper to Kate. "Can you really handle this gentleman?"

A deep masculine voice broke into the conversation, "Kate can handle almost anything...can't you dear?"

Kate smiled, hesitantly, offering her hand, "Hello, Craig. How are you?" she turned to Morgan, "Craig, my fiancé Morgan Buchanan."

The two men shook hands, warily assessing each other. Kate mentally compared the two, Morgan was taller and broader. Both had dark hair, their only similarity, Kate thought ruefully. Morgan's face though silent showed character, strength, purpose, ...Craig's slight beard covered a weak chin, his eyes narrowing slightly as he saw Kate's ring.

"Marrying for money?" He asked, his laugh sounding hollow to Kate.

Anger made her eyes flash as she picked up her wine glass ready to throw it, Morgan's hand quickly covering hers as he answered, "No, I'm in love with her. Kate," Morgan said sounding faintly amused, "You didn't tell me you were rich?"

"That's because you didn't ask," Kate replied matching his light words. A silent look passed between Morgan and Craig as dinner was finally served. Kate was proud of her performance as the loving fiancé, she didn't remember what she ate, the small talk, everything seemed a blur. Standing in the gardens later, she took a deep breath of cool, crisp evening air. Hearing steps behind her, Kate turned to stare as Craig approached; an unsmiling Kate tried to walk past him, the garden suddenly stifling as well. Craig's hand came out and grasped hers, pulling her towards him.

"Why Kate, Craig drawled, "I'd almost think you were trying to avoid me?"

"Then you think right," Kate answered trying to pull her arm free. His fingers only tightened over her bare arm. "We said

133

everything there was to say six years ago. My views haven't changed. Now let go of my arm... "

Craig's voice a sneer as he mimicked Kate, "Let go of my arm ..." He laughed, low menacing. "Not until I've gotten a proper welcome from you," and he pulled Kate closer into his arms. Kate could smell the alcohol on his breath, vaguely remembering his glass being filled and refilled during dinner.

"You disgust me," Kate said angrily, "I've asked you once, now I'm telling you let go of me or ..."

"Or what... You'll scream? You'll call for the doting fiancé?" He paused, "There's no big brother around to protect you, and this time you'll do what I say."

He lowered his head to kiss Kate, she stomped down using the heel of her shoe on his instep, his surprise, and momentarily loosening his hold, the only break Kate needed. When Morgan turned the corner in the garden, he heard Kate's voice low but angry, Craig's voice followed, Morgan bit out an angry expletive. He crossed the garden quickly only to find a stunned Craig lying helpless on the ground, a calmer, almost grinning Kate standing beside him.

" .. Or I'll take care of you myself!" Kate finished triumphantly. "Don't you ever touch me again, Mr. Warner... "Kate said only then seeing Morgan.

"Are you all right," Morgan asked taking in the situation, "Everything under control?"

Kate's relief was enormous, "Yes," she took the arm Morgan offered, "Just some old unfinished business."

"Just as long as he understands," No longer smiling, Morgan stared at Craig, "Next time I won't be quite as gentle at telling you as she was."

A mumbled yes from Craig and the two left to go inside. Kate could feel the anger making Morgan's arm tense.

"I can explain ..." she began.

"I know, and you will," Morgan said, as they said good night to their hosts and went back to their room, both were silent. With studied control, Morgan closed the bedroom door. Kate moved towards the bathroom, "I'll get ready..."

"Talk." Morgan finished, pulling her towards the bed. He sat her firmly down, looking with a darkening scowl at the red marks left by Craig's hands. "Who the hell is he Kate?" He bit out, gently rubbing her arms, almost as if to erase Craig's touch away.

"He... he used to be a friend of Danny's... "she began.

"Used to be?" he grunted.

At Kate's slight shake of her head, she continued, "When I came to live with the Ryan's when I was eighteen, we ... they made no secret as to where I had come from. I wasn't aware of some of the rumors being circulated about Da and my possible heritage." She blushed, not meeting Morgan's eyes. "With four brothers, one of them was always around. Craig... was one of their friends. He asked me out... "She paused; her hands clutched tightly together. "We dated, he was very nice until he decided he'd been good long enough and wasn't getting his full evening's worth, so to speak. My views and his didn't coincide." Pain crossed Kate's face remembering, "I lost my temper and struck him ..."

"He deserved it," bit out Morgan watching the pain.

"Yes," Kate laughed woodenly, "But he didn't think so and hit...hit me back." Morgan's hands stopped on her arms, his eyes boring into her, "He tore my dress before I managed to scream and get out of the car. He left me there told me to make my own way home, that maybe then I'd be ready to see things his way. He finished by telling me about Da and how I would never be anybody's wife, I wasn't good enough ..." Her voice trailed, tears falling softly down her cheeks.

Morgan gathered her into his arms, holding her, his hands gentle.

"When I got home..." Kate continued softly, "only Danny was awake, by then my face was swollen, my torn dress ... he thought I'd been raped." She paused again remembering, "It was all I could do assure him I was bruised but all right. He stayed home with me but next morning, he and Sean went to pay Craig a visit. He denied everything, of course, said I was a tease, led him on, surely, they knew how it was. Sean said he never got to finish his story. Danny had to be pulled off of him. They warned him if he ever came within a mile of me, they'd come back." She sniffed loudly. "Danny and Sean came home and my training in Judo began the same day. I learned quickly, Judo ... and not to tell people more than they needed to know. Not because I'm ashamed," she looked up at Morgan, her eyes bright with tears, "It was just easier. I became ..."

"...More secretive about your past," Morgan finished for her. "You know," he smiled, kissing her forehead protectively, "I like Dan more and more ..."

"You would," Kate said wryly.

Morgan smoothed back her hair, "I won't let him hurt you Kate." He assured her, and she believed him, with all her heart. "If you hadn't done such a good job on him, I would feel tempted to add my own touches."

"No!" Kate said, clutching at his shirt, "Please don't go. It's over," her tongue moistening her dry lips, "can't we just forget it?"

"Alright, little one," Morgan said, pulling Kate up, "you win, now let's get ready for bed, or couch, whatever you want to call it."

Kate laughed, "I feel mean making you take the couch, I'm shorter, why don't I take the couch?"

"No way," Morgan declared gathering up a pillow and a blanket from the foot of the bed. "Take the bathroom first, Red," he told her, and Kate went willingly, feeling very secure, almost loved, she said to herself, at least liked, she argued. Five minutes later, Kate stood at the bathroom door, still dressed, embarrassment staining her cheeks.

"What's wrong now, Kate," Morgan asked tying his own pajama bottoms on.

"Leigh made me bring everything," Kate said, "But we forgot ... a nightgown." she finished lamely.

Morgan's brows shot up, "A nightgown?" He asked, "No problem," He agreed a wicked grin appearing on his face. "Don' t wear one ... "

"Morgan!" Kate cried, "I can't ... not with you here... what do I do?" she wailed.

"Well since, I'm wearing the bottoms, you might as well wear the tops," He said tossing the cotton shirt at her. "Feel honored ... " he said laughing.

"Oh, I do," Kate assured him, "Thanks Morgan!"

"... that I even brought them. I usually don't." he finished wickedly.

"Then what?" Kate blushed, thinking of Morgan sleeping in the nude. "Luck was with me, yes?"

"Yes," Morgan said firmly, as the door shut. Minutes later, Kate opened the door and stood ready for inspection. The shirt while fitting Morgan, went far beneath Kate's knees, the sleeves had been rolled several times, and Kate had tied a belt around her waist.

"It certainly looks better on you, "Morgan decided liking what he saw.

"Morgan," Kate began hesitantly, "Do you think we could both sleep in the bed, just as friends?"

"Not on your life." Morgan said quietly. He crossed the room towards her, pulling her into his arms and kissing her once before pushing her gently away. His voice husky, deep with emotion, "I'm not lying beside you and not having you. I'm in control but I'm not made of stone, Red."

Kate nodded, understanding only all too well the dangerous pull between them. "Good night, Morgan," Kate said softly, tucked beneath the soft covers on the bed.

"Goodnight, little one," Morgan answered, his long, tall frame covering the couch.

Kate awoke to the running of the shower; she opened both eyes instantly looking for Morgan on the couch. Finding it empty, Kate smiled, she threw back the covers and walked over to the couch. The least I can do, she thought, is to make his bed. She threw the pillow back on the bed and deftly folded the blanket and put it back in the closet. She started to walk back to the bed when Morgan opened the bathroom door, a towel wrapped carelessly around his waist. He was using another to dry his hair.

"It's about time you're up!" he said smiling at the elflike image she was, "I figure you were going to sleep the day away."

Kate grinned and made a graceful pounce onto the bed, "Now that you've mentioned it, I think it sounds like a marvelous idea!"

"Oh, no you don't," Morgan chuckled flipping her gently with his free towel before sitting down on the bed. Morgan looked down at Kate, her hair still tousled from sleep, her eyes bright and sparkling, and one shoulder bare as the too large nightshirt slid down.

Morgan leant forward to pull it up, when there was a soft knock at the door and Marsha burst in, "Morgan?" she asked. Her hands holding a tray of coffee and two cups, she stared dumbfounded at the bed where Morgan and Kate lay. Morgan moved quickly, catching the tray before it fell to the floor.

"You slept with her!!" Marsha accused.

"You did put us in the same room ... one bed," Morgan said pointing out the facts.

"Yes, but ... but I expected ... I knew ... " she said her mind wheeling.

"Marsha," Morgan said firmly, "I told you and your dad before I came how things were between Kate and me."

"But I ... we thought it was all a game of yours to avoid... the merger ..."

"As you can see ..." Morgan said looking at Kate on the bed, not ending the sentence.

Marsha's eyes hardened, her hands knotted into fists, "I see more than you think, Morgan Buchanan," she said in a shrill voice and slammed the door.

"Coffee..." Morgan asked quietly.

"Please," Kate said her voice little more than a whisper. She could still see the hate on Marsha's face.

"Here you go little one, "Morgan said, handing her a cup, "Don't look so stricken, Kate, this is what we set out to do ... remember?"

Kate shook her head slowly, "I remember ... I just didn't plan on anyone getting hurt ..."

"Somebody's bound to be hurt when you try and force them into marriage. She'll be hurt a lot less now then if I did go through with it and the marriage was a disaster... as it was bound to be."

"What about Moreland Enterprises?"

"That's something that I should discuss with Mike today."

Kate laughed nervously at Morgan's questioning glance, "The sooner, the better..." "Well, between Craig and Marsha, I don't think we'll win any popularity polls," she added ruefully, "That only leaves Wanda Turner and Mike --Marsha's father ..."

"I'll go talk to him now," Morgan said, "as soon as I get dressed that is ..."

"I think that might help," Kate grinned mischievously, "unless, of course, you've changed your mind about Marsha?"

139

"Watch it, Red, "Morgan warned at the bathroom door, "I might throw you out to Craig's mercy."

"I'm quaking in my boots," Kate laughed.

Morgan appeared minutes later in dark slacks and a white shirt, his tan against the shirt looking darker than ever. Kate let out a low wolf whistle,

"Very nice, boss," she said teasingly.

"Glad you approve," Morgan mocked, walking over to where Kate sat. He kissed her without warning, his mouth moving, lingering against hers, "For luck," Morgan murmured, kissing her yet again.

"For luck... "Kate whispered responding yet wanting more. Morgan straightened, touching Kate's chin gently, he walked to the door and left.

Kate watched him go, she got up as the door closed and walked to the dresser mirror. Her eyes shining, Kate wondered if he could see the love in her face as plainly as she could. She grabbed her clothes and headed for the bathroom, determined to be ready when Morgan returned.

CHAPTER 12

Dressed in jeans and a cotton shirt, Kate was lacing her tennis shoes, when Morgan walked in the door, "Hey!" He said, " I thought you'd still be in bed!"

"Sorry to disappoint you, but ...," she grinned, "The great outdoors calls."

"Second place again," He laughed.

"Well, how did it go with Mike?" Kate looked down, thinking never second with me Morgan.

"Pretty well," He sat down beside Kate, "he's accepted I won't be his son-in-law for starters, and he's promised no delays in the parts that we've ordered." He pulled Kate's hair gently, "We're still talking about the device, and I'd say we have a fifty-fifty chance. Not bad considering how the day started ..."

"What's on the agenda for the rest of the day?" Kate asked her head resting on her knee.

"Mike mentioned a picnic lunch, bring your swimsuit, and a jacket, we're going by helicopter," He grabbed his own clothes, "I'll be ready in a minute."

Kate pulled out her suit from the bureau drawer, smiling at Morgan's enthusiasm, dreading another meeting with Marsha or Craig, yet with Morgan beside her, she knew she'd enjoy the afternoon.

Flying high above the treetops, Kate marveled at the great expanse of untouched forests that lay below. As far as the eye could see in all directions, rich timber lay. The sheltering limbs a haven for a multitude of feathered and furry friends. She smiled as she caught Morgan watching her. "What's wrong? Have I smudged my makeup?"

"No ... He returned her smile, "besides, you very seldom wear makeup."

"How do you know?" Kate asked startled.

"I know more about you than you think..." he replied.

"You think so?" Kate retorted, inwardly wondering how much he did know about her and her thoughts and her feelings...

Morgan just gave her a lazy warm smile, "Relax, Red, I don't see anything I don't like."

"Yes ..." Kate replied blushing, "How much farther do we go?"

"Changing the subject?"

"If I can ..." Kate admitted.

"I'll let you off the hook, this time..." Morgan said, turning to face Craig and Marsha. They were talking together on the other side of the helicopter; they looked up sharply, almost guiltily as Morgan repeated the question. "How much farther is the secret rendezvous?"

"We'll be there soon," Marsha replied, "its many miles from the cottage, by air only a few hours away, unfortunately by foot it would take several days."

"It's a good thing we've got the 'copter then," Morgan replied hoping to maintain cordial relations with Marsha, regardless of the morning's confrontation.

"I've heard tell of people being lost for days in these woods." Craig said casually, "Maybe even weeks before they're found." He smiled, although it reminded Kate more of a sneer.

A chill crept up her back; she shook her head to clear up her feelings of apprehension. The rest of the journey was flown in silence. Their pilot set down the helicopter gently atop a small hill. As they climbed out, Morgan and Kate volunteered to help carry the picnic supplies. Grabbing her backpack in one arm and a thermos in the other, Kate followed Morgan and the hamper of food. Craig and Marsha were following behind.

Hearing the helicopter again, Morgan turned to wave to their pilot. He stopped and yelled, dropping the basket, he began running back to the clearing. Only then did Kate turn in puzzlement to where Morgan was heading. By then it was too late, their transportation along with their hosts had again taken off, leaving a very puzzled Kate, and a furious Morgan.

"...of all the ..." Morgan's anger was directed at Marsha and Craig and at the moment anything within earshot.

Kate walked back to the hamper Morgan had dropped, looking inside she took a quick assessment of their supplies. Piling everything together, she turned back to Morgan.

He was quiet now, his hands deep in his pockets, "Morgan?" Kate spoke softly.

He turned towards her instantly, his eyes in agony, his mouth set ..."Don't worry, Kate, I won't let you get hurt. I'll get us out of here somehow." He reached up to touch her chin, "My God! What could they have been thinking of?! If they want me lost ... fine! But not you ..." his voice broke off.

"We're a package deal, remember?" Kate reminded him gently.

"I'm sorry I ever got you into this, Kate." He pulled her to him, and held her, his hand gently forming circles on her back. "How can I expect to get through this forest with you ..." he spoke to himself more than to Kate, "Maybe ... we'll rig up a shelter, you'll stay here, and I'll go for help ..." His hands shook, "But I can't leave you here alone! Damn!" He cursed low beneath his breath,

Kate's shoulders, had begun to shake" Don't cry, Red, I'll get us out of this mess."

"Idiot," Kate laughed out loud, "I'm not crying!"

"Well, I sure as hell don't see anything to laugh about!" Morgan retorted.

"No, I know you don't "Kate said, touched by his concern for her. On impulse she reached up and kissed him, "Thanks for caring about me," she whispered.

"Now," she said, "Let's eat over by the stream. We'll talk over what it is we have to do and then do it."

"It's not that simple," Morgan said, following behind Kate reluctantly, picking up the hamper again. "There's about two hundred miles of forest out there. Experienced men could hike out in a few days, but we're not experienced and one of us is not a man ... "He brushed Kate's objections aside, "she's five feet, barely a hundred pounds and a woman, my woman, and I don't want to see her hurt!!"

"Morgan," Kate began touching his arm as she spoke, "I've been living in the woods most of my life and I'm not made of porcelain. I can manage just fine. I promise." She paused, smiling, dimples showing beneath shining eyes, "You lead, and I'll follow, only don't take very big steps, my legs aren't as long as yours, ok?"

Morgan looked at Kate for a long time, taking in all five feet of her, he drew a deep breath, exhaling slowly as if purging his very soul. "You're quite a girl, Kate," he said as last.

CHAPTER 13

Carefully storing the equipment, they would need, Kate fit each piece in her well-worn backpack. Slipping on their swimsuits and then dressing again gave them the extra room needed. Kate mentally listed each supply as she packed it, thermos, vinyl tablecloth, blanket, salt and pepper, silverware, plates (metal, thank heaven!), two towels, and a few plastic bags left from their picnic hamper. She turned to Morgan who had been silently watching the rushing water of the stream. "Ready, when you are, Morgan," she said standing.

"If we follow the stream, we'll be by fresh water and closest to any other travelers. But if it winds, it may take us longer. If we go cross country, it'll be shorter, but I can't guarantee fresh water ... We can go for a while without food but not water ... Although longer it'll be safest if we travel downstream ... Does that sound alright, Kate?" Morgan asked.

"You're the boss," Kate grinned, "besides you've got the supplies, I'll follow you anywhere!"

Morgan picked up the backpack, adjusting the straps for his much broader chest and back. "Let's go." He said solemnly, looking again at Kate, "Let me know if you get tired, we'll rest, agreed?"

"Agreed..." Kate said meeting Morgan's cautious look.

Morgan chose a path about ten feet away from the stream, close enough to follow it but far enough away to avoid the thick brush that lined its banks. He set a brisk pace but constantly watched Kate for any signs of fatigue. After about an hour, Morgan called a halt to rest for a bit and took a drink of water as well.

"We're traveling southwest," Kate remarked sinking down to sit cross legged in front of Morgan, "Do you think this will flow into the Mississippi?"

Morgan raised one eyebrow, "What leads you to believe we're traveling southwest, Kate?"

"Moss grows on the north side of the trees," she replied matter of fact, "just deductive reasoning."

"Good deduction, directionally anyway, " Morgan smiled, his first since they had been left, "but I doubt this small stream flows into the Mississippi, not directly at any rate. This probably flows into a tributary of the big muddy." He sighed, "Unfortunately, there could be miles of stream before we get there."

"And miles to go before we sleep" Kate finished for him, quoting from Robert Frost's poem.

"Break's over," Morgan said, pulling Kate to her feet, and he again set off. His silence didn't bother her; she knew his mind was concerned with her and their safety, food, nightfall... Poor Morgan, Kate sighed, how do I convince you we'll be fine? You keep brushing aside my capabilities. I guess I just show you that there's always food in a forest such as this. Shelter's not a problem and hiking for days or weeks didn't really worry her, it simply meant more time to spend with Morgan.

Untying her jacket from around her waist, Kate slipped it on. Not to keep warm, she was already perspiring from the damp, humid undergrowth created by the June sun, but to protect her arms from the brush as well as the bites of insects. They rested several more times, before Morgan decided they should set up camp for the night. Telling Kate to just rest, he took off to survey their surroundings. Left on her own, Kate decided to surprise Morgan with a campsite and dinner when he returned.

Kate gathered a pile of dry leaves and grass. She took a string off her shirt. Tying it to a stick, she made a bow. She took a short stick and turned it around the string. Putting the sticks into a pile of leaves, she began rubbing them together; soon, she had a fire going.

One down, thought Kate, eying the young sapling before her. Taking out her shoestrings, she leaned against the small willowy trunk until its tip almost touched the ground. Slipping a knot first around the top and then anchoring it to a nearby bush. She spread more limbs across the boughs of the tree until, her lean-to was finished.

Not bad, Kate giggled, wondering what Morgan's reaction was going to be. And now for step three, Kate said, walking down to the bank whistling. Using a stick, Kate whittled out a sharp end. Crouching low over some rocks, Kate watched for movement in the stream bed. Hoping her reflexes would be fast enough, remembering how long she and her brothers had had to wait before actually being able to spear their own dinner...

When Morgan returned sometime later, he was hot, thirsty and very worried about Kate. He carried in his shirt a pile of mulberries, wild onions, and mushrooms. Not much, he decided, but they wouldn't go to sleep hungry. Poor Kate, he thought, he'd been gone for some time. Time enough for her to lose her brave front of not being afraid. The smell of smoke caused Morgan to hurry through the brush, "Kate?" he called, puzzled by the silence. "Kate?!" he raised his voice.

"Supper will be ready in about five minutes," Kate called back, "Time enough to wash up in the stream."

"What do you mean supper ..." he began a he broke through the underbrush. He stopped in his tracks.

Kate knelt before a fire, cooking what looked like fish over the fire on splits. Behind her was a rough lean-to, their vinyl tablecloth spread under it. Their pillows were rolled up beach towels.

"Who ... what ... how?" Morgan began looking in wonder at the campsite and Kate.

"I tried to tell you not to worry about me, I've been camping all my life, usually with a little more gear but making do was always part of the game."

Still Morgan was silent, Kate hesitated, worried that she had hurt his masculine pride. "Morgan?" Kate said, standing up and walking over to touch his arm almost to break his trance.

"You are unbelievable," Morgan said slowly, shaking his head, "Just when I think I have you all figured out, you do something totally out of character." He handed Kate his shirt, smiling at her smudged nose and unruly hair, "What miracles can you work with them?"

"Depends what they are ..." Kate said embarrassed at the look Morgan threw her way. "Go ahead and wash up," she said mumbling as she opened his shirt and found the fruit and vegetables. She quickly placed one of the metal plates beneath the fish, their natural oil, sizzling onto the fire. Now the oil fell drop by drop onto the plate, Kate washed the food and placed the onions and mushrooms to simmer on the plate. The berries she washed and set aside on another of the plates. Morgan watched her work, her hands small but sure moving from task to task. He walked the short distance to the water and knelt, rinsing his hands and face in the cool refreshing spray. He hastened back to camp, only to find Kate placing their evening's meal onto a plate.

"It's not Cordon Bleu," Kate said almost as an apology, "But" she grinned impishly, "its eatable."

"It sure smells fantastic," Morgan said, sliding down beside Kate. But even his eyes opened wide in surprise after his first bite. "It's delicious!" he exclaimed, much to Kate's delight.

"Don't sound so surprised," Kate laughed, very pleased at his reaction.

"But this is really good," Morgan went on, "Even camp cooking was never like this!"

"Thanks," said Kate, biting into her own fish.

"Now for the million-dollar question, how did you do all..." He waved his free hand around the camp, "this ...?"

"Growing up in the hills of Missouri, all of this, was what I did all year, a lot of it was experimental, you, know, Pat or Sean would read something in a book, Mike would hear what somebody else did and at that time Danny loved Indians ... we read, we tried, Bingo, this campsite is the result of years of summers with the Ryan's." Kate was silent, remembering. "... The first million times we ever tried spear fishing was a disaster. We speared everything from tires to frogs and once Dan even speared his own foot!" She burst out laughing, "I think that must have been what started Mike's medical career and almost ended our 'Green Beret training' as Sean used to call it!" She stopped, not wanting to bore Morgan with her childhood.

"You still manage to surprise me," Morgan leaned back on one elbow. "You look like a strong wind would carry you away, but you stand up to me and Craig and four extremely big brothers."

"Stand up?" Kate grunted, "I just don't let you always have your own way!"

"Maybe so," Morgan agreed, gently pulling her hair. "Now, not to change the subject but how do we wash the dishes?"

"Bring your plate and follow me," Kate laughed leading him back to the stream. "Wash it by turning sand from the bottom of the creek on the plate, the sand cleans it, the creek washes and rinses all in a few easy swishes," she explained.

"Swishes...?" Morgan asked in the dark clear night.

"Swishes..." Kate answered firmly, taking his big hands between her own and demonstrating. "Now wasn't that easy?" Kate said quickly drawing away from the almost electric touch of his hands.

"It's almost as easy as throwing them in the dish washer at home."

"Come on," Kate teased, "You don't expect me to believe you wash dishes, even use a dishwasher...?"

"More than you might think," Morgan responded, "there were many lean years working two jobs, maids don't grow on trees you know!"

"Maids, I agree," Kate agreed solemnly, "But I'm sure there were plenty of girls willing to playhouse and do them for you!"

Morgan splashed at Kate, "That's for being impertinent, young lady."

"Not impertinent," Kate splashed back, and ran back towards camp, "just stating facts," she yelled over her shoulder in parting.

Morgan followed behind her, Kate banked the fire and threw some leaves on as well, "The smoke should keep us from getting too bug bit," Kate explained, as she spread Morgan's shirt over a bush to dry. She looked up, nervous at finding Morgan watching her. "Why...don't you go on to bed," She swallowed avoiding his eyes, "I think I'll sit and watch the fire a bit..."

"Kate," Morgan began, sitting down beside her, "I'm not going to ravish you simply because we have to sleep together. Not that I wouldn't want to," he added, devilishly, "But being on the hard ground, with all our clothes on in the middle of a forest should keep you safe, then again," He paused, "If you remember, I asked you to trust me ... "

"I do ..." Kate replied softly.

"Well then, young lady," Morgan said holding out his hand to Kate, "its bedtime and we've a long way to go." He pulled Kate to her feet with one swift pull, throwing her against him. Instinctively Kate reached out to hold onto him, to catch herself. Morgan's arms tightened drawing her even closer, a low moan escaped Morgan and then his lips were on hers. Seconds later, Morgan gently raised his head; he kissed the tip of Kate's nose and said huskily, "That was a goodnight kiss ..."

"Oh ... "Kate replied, her own voice shaking, "I wondered about that ..."

Slowly, almost reluctantly Morgan let go of her, following her to her lean-to. Lying on the vinyl tablecloth, covered with the blanket, Morgan's nearness was almost overpowering. Kate's rapid breath mirrored her confused mind, her senses wanting more. Oh my God, Kate wondered, how am I ever going to sleep with him so near. I can feel the warmth of his body...

"Go to sleep, Kate," Morgan said, breaking the silence.

"I'm trying," Kate said, rolling over again, "I'm not used to ... anyone being so close when I sleep," she finished rolling yet again.

"Good," Morgan growled, seizing the turning Kate and pulling her closer to him. She tensed, "Relax, Red, I'm just going to position us so we can both get some sleep." He pulled Kate close beside him, resting his arm beneath her head, placing her head on his shoulder. Her body turned as if coming home, curling up beside him. "Now," Morgan said touching her hair with his lips, his arm holding her protectively, "Go to sleep ..."

"Yes sir," Kate whispered, already half asleep.

Morgan listened for her slow even breathing to know she was asleep. His hand moved gently against her back. He pulled the blanket up around her and closed his own eyes as well but sleep for Morgan was a long while in coming.

Kate woke early, the morning shimmering in the early dew. She gently eased herself from Morgan's arm, watching him, as he slept. Sighing softly, Kate stood up, stretching her arms high above her head. She put fresh wood on the fire and walked towards the stream. Splashing water on her face, Kate began a quick search for their morning's breakfast.

Morgan awoke to the smell of coffee simmering. He smiled, then remembered where he was. His arms were empty. Raising himself on one elbow, he saw Kate grinning, kneeling beside the fire.

"It's about time!" She cried. "I've been up for quite some time."

"I had trouble getting to sleep ..." Morgan said, rising quickly, his eyes never leaving Kate's face. Understanding the reason why, Kate blushed. He continued. "I could swear I could smell coffee. Don't tell me you've managed that in your bag of tricks, too?"

"Almost..." Kate laughed taking one of the metal plates off the fire and pouring it into the thermos cup. "Try it," she told him as she passed it to Morgan.

"Not bad," Morgan said approvingly. "Not coffee?" he said questioningly. "But it tastes very similar. Is it safe to ask what it is?"

"Yes." Kate said spooning up his plate with breakfast. "It's chicory. Back in the hills, they use it in place of coffee. Coffee is an added extravagance. Chicory on the other hand...is free and can be found in almost any woods."

"And this ...?" Morgan said looking at his plate of onions, mushrooms, and an animal-definitely not fish.

"Crayfish, crawdads" Kate informed him. "They're considered a delicacy in New Orleans, just plain country fair back home." She broke open the shell, showing Morgan the meat inside. "They're supposed to be simmered in butter, but I couldn't conjure up that ...”

"They're good," Morgan said, "definitely edible anyway ... " he teased.

"Eat hardy," Kate warned, "We're eating the mulberries you picked yesterday for lunch and whatever else I can see, that way we can make better time, OK?"

"I don't know ..."Morgan said, taking Kate's plate as well as his own down to the creek to wash them. Kate followed puzzled by his words. "I just might decide to settle here permanently," He said, his eyes hooded by the sun, "It'll be like Robinson Caruso, you'll be my woman Friday. All the comforts of home, with none of the problems ...”

"Oh, no you don't," Kate said smiling. "It sounds more like you Indian chief, and me Indian squaw! You do the relaxing, me the work!!"

"You don't like the idea?" Morgan grinned walking back to camp.

"Definitely not," Kate assured him, packing up the supplies, and handing the backpack to Morgan. She crossed to the sapling she had tied to form the lean-to; she put her shoelaces back in her shoes, she carefully slipped the knot and it quickly sprang back to its original height. Crossing to the fire, Kate spread the coals still hot, and poured water from the thermos on them; she then covered the embers with dirt. When she was satisfied that the fire was well and truly out, she straightened, looked around, content they were leaving the campsite as they had found it.

"Ready?" Morgan questioned, watching Kate with respect.

"Ready!" Kate confirmed again following as Morgan led through the thick underbrush. His pace was faster today, a growing confidence in Kate's capabilities and the question of her able to keep up no longer a problem.

The day stretched on almost endlessly, Morgan drove them further and further. His eyes were ever watchful of Kate and changes around them. Their short rest at lunch, another a few hours later, by late afternoon even Kate was showing signs of wear. Most of their walking had been done in silence; both needed their breath strictly for their brisk pace.

"Morgan?" Kate called out finally, "Whatever are we racing to?"

He turned to watch her, coming towards him, her face flushed from the day's hike, her shirt clinging to her damp body. He saw the signs of fatigue on her face. Morgan pointed to the sky, and frowned, "I've been trying to out walk the storm." The dark clouds a threatening presence.

"I saw them," Kate said, "and felt the still humid air. I've been in storms before, Morgan. We'll be okay; we just need to find shelter."

"I've been looking" Morgan said, his hand going through his hair in frustration, "The entire day I've been searching for a cave, anything to shelter us. Your lean-to was great. "He smiled his teeth even white against his dark skin, "But not hardy enough to withstand a real cloudburst ..."

"No," Kate said, returning his smile, "But had you mentioned your concern, I could have helped you look. Four eyes are better than two?"

"You've done enough," Morgan countered, his admiration showing, "I didn't want to worry you ..."

"Right," Kate laughed, shaking her head and looking about, "We'll both worry later, now to find shelter." She headed towards the bank of the creek. "Over there," Kate pointed across the water, "You can see how high the creek rises during a rain, above the banks on the left is a hollow. Some animal probably used it as a den." She turned to Morgan, "It'll be cramped but it should be dry..."

"Fantastic!" Morgan said his arms swinging down to lift Kate in his arms and walking down to the water and wading in.

"Hey! Put me down!" Kate squealed, turning in his arms, he laughed at her efforts, only tightening his hold.

"All in good time," He said crossing easily to the other side and depositing Kate safely to the ground. "Now we'll make camp and get situated early, I don't think we've got much time to spare."

"But why carry me across?" Kate stood hands on her hips, demanding from him an answer. In turn Morgan pulled her roughly into his arms and kissed her. Releasing her slowly, "I just wanted to feel you in my arms again, little one," Morgan said quietly. "You could become an addicting habit," he finished, turning towards the hollow before she could answer. After depositing her knapsack at the base of the den, he asked, "What can I do to help?"

Kate pulled herself together, her mind and thoughts on the feel of Morgan's hands on the meaning of his words. Is there hope for me after all, Kate wondered hopefully. Organizing Morgan, Kate had him collect some firewood while she set about trying to again spear their supper, ever watching the darkening rolling sky. Laying down her catch, Kate dug down and pulled a few cattail roots from the ground. She headed for the hollow. Morgan had just returned, stacking a good supply of dry wood against the walls.

"I don't know about you," Kate began, "But before it storms, I'd like a wash in that stream. There's a breeze picking up, if we wash out our clothes, they'll have a chance to dry before the downpour." She raised questioning brows to Morgan.

"What about a fire?"

"With the wood and a pile of dried leaves even in a storm we'll be fine."

"All right then you're on, "Morgan agreed, "I'll get some leaves and meet you down by the water. Clean clothes sure sound good," He laughed looking at their grubby appearance, "I think right now, they'd stand up by themselves!"

Kate laughed, "I Agree!!" she started for the bank, "Hurry" she yelled over her shoulder, all too aware of him in the small hollow space. Taking off her shirt, slacks and socks, Kate jumped into the cool water, reveling in its refreshing feeling. Shaking the water from her hair, she swam back to shore to wash it against the rocks and sand. "That'll do ..." Kate decided, spreading them over a branch to dry in the breeze. "Morgan?" Kate yelled, startled to find him behind her, just watching her, "Better give me your clothes," She said, her eyes mesmerized by his lean torso, his powerful arms and legs. An Adonis, Kate said to herself, never more aware of the effect his presence had over her. Still Morgan stood there, taking in the sight of Kate, her simple maillot suit, showing her body's curves and secrets. "Morgan...?" she asked again nervously.

"You're perfect, you know," Morgan finally answered handing his clothes to her.

"You haven't always thought so," Kate teased afraid of his serious tone, not yet prepared for his answers.

"Yes ..." Morgan said, taking his cue from her light tone. "I know but, now I've decided if ever we should get stranded in a forest again, you're definitely my number #1 choice for a companion."

"Thanks, I think," Kate said, her head bent over his clothes to hide her feelings.

Morgan dove into the water, splashing at Kate bent over her task. "They're not great," Kate admitted ruefully, "But better than they were!" She threw them over the limb, as well, the breeze increasing as the storm drew nearer.

156

"Remind me to take a tree limb into the cave as we leave." Kate called out to Morgan.

"What for?"

"Just remind me. Ok?"

"You got it. Red." he smiled coming up behind her and ducking her under.

"There goes your supper." Kate warned shaking a finger at a laughing Morgan.

"I hear you," Morgan said as Kate dove under water to help make him lose his balance. Grabbing hold of his left leg, Kate pushed, and succeeded in tumbling Morgan's great bulk into the water. Like children they splashed and swam enjoying the relaxing play in the water. All too soon thunder echoed through the trees. Morgan pulled a reluctant Kate from the water, their clothes were still damp as they gathered them up along with their shoes and headed for the cave, remembering to bring the branch Kate had mentioned.

Once inside, Morgan helped Kate start the fire, and begin their supper. The fish once again cooked on splits. Kate placed a plate with water in it under them; into the water she placed the cattail roots.

"Trust me ..." Kate assured a puzzled Morgan at her culinary efforts, "I know what I'm doing!"

"I believe you," Morgan laughed, "I just never fail to be amazed at your ingenuity!"

"Good," Kate said pleased at her success, "Men love a woman of mystery and surprise; now help me with this tablecloth."

"We're going to eat on a tablecloth?"

"Not exactly," Kate explained, "It's the only thing waterproof we've got, if we hang it over the doorway, most of the rain will stay out, the fire will keep us dry and the heat should dry our clothes, provided we ... "

"...hang them over the tree limbs." Morgan finished for her, "Very clever, Miss O'Hara, remind me to give you a raise when we get back, you've definitely earned it ..."

Kate was silent, adjusting the clothes on the makeshift clothesline. "I don't work for you anymore, Morgan, you ... you have a new secretary, Mrs. Ross ... remember?"

"I remember," Morgan said flatly, finishing the door in silence.

Kate rolled out their blanket and handed Morgan his towel, using her own to briskly dry her hair and legs. When she finished feeling very self-conscience of the small space and wearing only her swimsuit, Kate wrapped the towel like a sarong around herself. Morgan watched her; his own towel used roughly across his back, his chest, and then hung around his shoulders. In the small firelit cave, their shadows danced upon the walls. Never was Kate more aware of Morgan's presence or his magnetism.

"Dinner's ready," she announced, slipping one of the fish and some cattail roots onto Morgan's plate.

"Are you going to tell me before or after I take a bite of the green stuff what it is?" He asked, raising questioning dark eyes to Kate's emerald ones.

"Definitely after," Kate said smiling impishly, the tension somehow easing over the sharing of a meal.

"Alright, here goes..." and Morgan bravely bit into the young green roots. Chewing carefully, he again looked up at Kate, "Hey! They're not bad," He said surprised.

Kate's golden laugh echoed through the cave, "Good boy! Those are cattails by the way; Russians have been eating them for years because of the starch they contain. The English call them Cossack asparagus." She bit into her own, "Not equal to a baked potato, but a help in trying to keep you properly fed!"

Morgan smiled, "Well, keep up the good work, Kate. I approve of the menus so far."

"Good, because they'll probably be the same menu's you'll get in the future, too!"

They were interrupted by the beginning rain, drops at first, settling the dust only minutes before it seemed as if the very sky had opened up. The water ran in sheets down the tablecloth and on down towards the bank. Kate sighed, inside their hollow. It felt good to be safe and dry. However, cramped they were, with the storm raging their haven seemed very cozy. Kate took the plates and let the rain wash them by setting them outside the cave for a few minutes. She set them around the campfire to dry them, and then she put them back in her backpack. The air was becoming cooler; Kate checked their clothes, glad when they were dry. Handing Morgan his, they dressed in silence. Kate hung their damp towels on the branches and stoked the fire, creating a steady heat in the cave as well as a dim glow of light.

"We might as well sack out," Morgan said, crossing to the blanket, "If we lie very close, we'll be able to use half of it as a bottom, the other half as our top, with our own body heat ..." he grinned, "You'll be snug as a bug... "

"...in a rug." Kate finished, nervously. All day she had looked forward to spending another night in Morgan's arms. Crawling beneath the blanket and being pulled close to Morgan as he tucked the edges under, Kate's heart quickened.

"Relax, Red," Morgan murmured, again drawing her against his shoulder, his arm protectively around her. "Try and get some sleep," He gently kissed Kate's forehead, "Goodnight."

"Goodnight, "Kate echoed very secure in Morgan's arms. Contentment washed over her tired aching muscles. She listened to Morgan's even, steady breathing. How many more days do I have, Kate wondered, before you kiss me good-by and disappear from my life. She thought of the many hours she spent alone in her own cabin, knowing that she would never again fish beside her own creek without remembering Morgan. Every walk through the woods would bring up his image. Kate shivered, causing Morgan to tighten his arm, even in his slumber protecting her. Oh, Morgan ... Morgan, how am I to live without you? I will survive, Kate knew with a certainty that chilled her, but the joy she had always felt with life would be gone. She wondered about Morgan, would he miss me, think about me? Probably with a smile as he remembered the Red shrew who once cooked him fish. But he'll get on with his life, as I must Kate resolved. She stole a look at Morgan's profile, his dark hair falling across his forehead, the straight nose, almost aristocratic, the stubble of beard covering his chin. His lips were almost sensuous, Kate thought, smiling to herself, just thinking about the touch of his lips against hers made her blush. I love you Morgan, Kate said to herself, I may never be able to tell you, but I love you. I will love you today, and all the tomorrows I shall live. Perhaps one day I shall love again, but you shall still be there, an ever-present shadow. A reminder that I was capable of a love of such intense feeling, Kate closed her eyes, feeling the tears brim over and fall slowly down her cheeks.

Still the rain fell, its soft patter against the door of their hollow, an easing sound. Continuous, almost hypnotic, Kate finally slept. By morning the rain had stopped, left in its aftermath was a world freshly washed and sparkling like a thousand diamonds on the leaves of trees, bushes, and a multitude of grass blades. Each seemed to have drunk thirstily of the night's shower and reveled in its purity. The colors of every flower seemed brighter. Kate drew back the vinyl doorway, shaking the excess moisture from it as she spread it to dry. The creek had risen during the night, overflowing from the many underground rivulets all leading to the stream. Running high, many branches were being carried downstream by the swiftly moving water. Smiling to herself she walked down to the bank. I wonder what treasures the muddy waters will carry away,

Kate wondered remembering the lucky finds she had fished out of the water after heavy rains back home. She began digging for crawfish again, knowing the muddy water would be very hard to catch fish for breakfast.

"Kate!" Morgan called from the cave's entrance, smiling broadly as he watched her crouching beside the water's edge. He started down whistling to himself, Kate smiled at his exuberance. Halfway down the bank Morgan began running and shouting at Kate, "help catch it Kate before we lose it!"

Puzzled Kate frowned, trying to figure out what he meant. She looked towards the stream where Morgan was heading and dropped her catch with a gasp and dove into the water. The current was much stronger due to the rain, but Kate managed to swim towards the craft coming downstream. She reached for the rope hanging from the bow of the canoe, just as Morgan reached her side. Together they pulled and guided the boat ashore. Exhausted Kate leaned against the bank still holding the rope in her hands as Morgan pulled the canoe further out of the water to insure its capture. He walked around it, checking for any possible leaks or breaks in its structure.

"Well," Kate asked, "what do you think? Is it seaworthy?"

"I think we're in business," Morgan said sitting down beside her, "Where'd she come from?"

"Probably broke off during the storm," she handed Morgan the frayed rope, "A lot of people go on float trips on these rivers, usually on the bigger ones but it's not unheard of to go down the smaller ones especially if you're a beginner ..."

"Which means," Morgan continued as he watched her concern, "that there are beginners hiking upstream someplace ..."

"Yep," Kate said, "Chances are at least one person in their group is experienced, he'll start them down the stream by shifting loads to accommodate for the lost canoe. On the other hand, it just might be a couple of kids on their own and they've just lost their main transportation."

"Well, do we leave it here or do we borrow it?" Morgan asked.

Kate sat up, her arms resting on her knees, "We take it," she said finally, "and we send back some help for whoever lost the canoe," she went on almost as an apology for her decision, "We'll make better time in the canoe than on foot and we'll be able to send help sooner."

"Agreed," Morgan said solemnly, standing and reaching down to help Kate up. "Let's get moving the sooner we start, the sooner we'll be there."

Kate nodded, still thinking of the boat's previous owners. Together they loaded up their gear, abandoning any efforts for breakfast. As they stowed the knapsack between them, Kate took the bow of the canoe, leaving Morgan to steer at the stern. The wooden paddles which had been secured beneath the seats skimmed the water gracefully as Kate and Morgan set off. Kate was never more aware of the beauty around them, trudging through the woods beside Morgan had left very little time to enjoy their surroundings. Their heavy walking had scared most of the wildlife away, now the almost silent strokes were all the noise made. Curious woodland creatures were all out to drink from the stream. Raccoons were busy washing their food, the black eyes covered by their masks. Further down the stream, a startled doe raised velvet brown eyes to stare at their approaching craft. Her small spotted fawn standing on wobbly legs beside her. Kate sighed, wishing she had brought her camera to capture the peace and harmony of the river life. Kate began humming, softly the music barely audible, and the tunes keeping her strokes smooth and sure.

"I recognize some of those," Morgan said quietly listening, relaxed as the river carried them farther downstream.

"If you know them, "Kate said, smiling back at him, "Then join in, you can't have an Irish 'ceill' with only one person."

"A 'ceill'?"

"An Irish party," Kate informed him, "You sing songs, have stories and if you're lucky you get someone to do some dances-like the Irish jig... "

"Not me!" Morgan laughed, "At least the jig part. Tell me about the stories, about Finn somebody, the whole lot of them."

Kate made a grimace, "You've been talking to Danny, and he's the real storyteller or 'seneschal' as they're called in Gaelic. Anything worth remembering is to be put in the form of a story or verse."

"Who was he?" Morgan asked again, watching the graceful way Kate maneuvered the paddle almost effortlessly.

"Are you sure you really want to know," Kate asked, "It's a rather long story."

"I've got all day," Morgan said wryly, "I don't believe I have any other pressing engagements," He grinned, "I'll even tell my secretary to hold all calls while you give me a condensed version, I'll even try and amaze Danny at my knowledge next time we meet."

"That'll be the day," Kate laughed, "You will be his friend for life, though." She paused, "All right, the condensed version... well to begin with, there are two cycles Irish legends fall into. The Ulster cycle centers on the ancient kingdom of Ulster and its hero Cúchulalnm, who could change into a dragon or defeat a thousand warriors single handedly ..."

"Sounds like a worthy fellow to have around." Morgan agreed solemnly, his dark eyes twinkling.

"Yes, I'm sure," Kate said, leaning back as they rounded a curve, "The Filian cycle is about the adventures of a band of warriors called the Fiana. It's leader Finn McCumhail, and his son

Oisin." Kate smiled, "When we were kids, Danny was always Finn, because I had hair the same color and because nobody else would be his son, I was always Oisin, Mike, Sean, and Pat our trusty warriors."

Morgan chuckled, "Where do all the leprechauns come in?"

"I'm coming to that," Kate laughed, "Be patient! Not all tales had fairy folk, in Gaelic, fairies, are called 'sidhe'. It means people of the mounds. Irish fairies are put into two groups, those who live and travel in groups and are generally considered to be good ..."

"Like the shoemaker's elves," Morgan offered, enjoying Kate's story.

"Right!" Kate said, glad to know Morgan was listening, "Solitary fairies are often greedy and mean, leprechauns for example. Other fairy folk include the pooka, they assume the shape of a horse; a banshee, whose cry foretells a death; the cluricann," she wrinkled her forehead in thought, trying to remember them all, "they're a tiny household elf; the merrow Thichis like a mermaid; the gruagach, " She looked up at Morgan's big form, "That's like you or in simple terms a giant," Kate added mischievously, "and of course the beasts or serpents of the lakes."

"I'm impressed, Morgan said, "Where'd you learn all the information, or did you take a course in Irish Folklore?"

"It wasn't necessary," Kate smiled, "When most Irish came to America, they had very few material possessions, but they carried in their heads a wealth of legends and fairy tales. Seanachai were respected and an essential part of any important gathering. Everything was passed on from generation to generation by word of mouth. If you hear it over and over in front of a fire, you remember." For a time, Kate was silent, remembering Da as they had sat before the campfire and his tales of Finn. Kate had never tired of his stories. She shook her head, "I'll bet you didn't know that a lot of Irish traditions are no longer thought of as Irish," she challenged.

"Such as?"

"The Irish were the first to set out jack-a-lanterns and to trick or treating on Halloween. The lucky horseshoe and the custom of a bride wearing something old, something new, something borrowed, something blue to name a few," Kate finished triumphantly.

"I give up," Morgan said, throwing his hands up in mock surrender.

"Good," Kate said impishly, "I've about said all I know on the subject! I was worried I'd run out of things to say!"

"That'll be the day," Morgan said using his paddle to lightly splash Kate's back.

"Two can play that game," Kate warned as she cupped her hand to splash him back. Her eyes on Morgan, she failed to look in the water.

"Kate! No! "Morgan shouted as he leaned forward to pull her hand from the side of the boat.

Kate's puzzlement turned to pain, as the snake buried its fangs deep into her arm ... Seconds too late Morgan pulled Kate's arm from the water, the snake disappearing quickly silently through the water. Kate looked at the two crimson marks on her arm; tears filled her eyes as she thought frantically as to what she should do next. Shock turned her normally decisive movements clumsy.

CHAPTER 14

With sure strokes, Morgan took the canoe to the shore, jumping out and pulling high up on the beach. He bent beside the still kneeling Kate.

"Where's your pocketknife, Kate?" He said, tearing his shirt and tying a tourniquet above Kate's elbow.

"What ...?" Kate asked almost bemused, still staring at the tiny marks.

"Your knife!" Morgan shouted in exasperation and fear. His hand was already pulling the knife from the pocket of her jeans. He made two small cuts above each mark causing Kate to wince. She bit her lip to keep from crying out. Morgan's forehead creased above his eyes bent on his task but straying constantly to Kate's ashen face.

"I'm sorry Red." Morgan said his voice little more than a murmur as he put his mouth over the incision to draw the poison form her veins.

Kate stayed very still common sense telling her to remain as quiet as possible but even in her pain the feel of Morgan's lips against her skin caused her to shiver.

Working feverishly over her arm, Morgan stopped and laid Kate down in the canoe, using the knapsack as a pillow and covering her with the blanket to ward off the reaction he knew she would feel.

"You'll be all right, little one," Morgan said, tucking the blanket around her body, "Did you see what kind of snake it was, Kate?"

Numbly she nodded her head, "A cottonmouth," she whispered, "Water moccasin, they're the same thing..." her voice trailed.

Morgan bent and kissed Kate's trembling lips, "Don't worry Red, I won't let anything happen to you, trust me ..." He said firmly.

A shaky smile came from Kate as she watched his worried face, "I promised I would, remember?" she asked.

"I remember," Morgan smiled back, his hand going out involuntarily to touch her cheek, "I'm putting us back in the water, Kate, and I'll go nonstop. You have to lay quiet, understand?"

Nodding her head, yes, Morgan whispered in determination, "That's my girl..."

He pushed off, taking care not to disturb Kate as he climbed in. This time his oars dug deep into the water; his pace steady, almost fevered as he watched Kate fall asleep the discoloration of her arm growing darker. He loosened the tourniquet for a few minutes only to retie it, he touched her hair once before again he pushed himself on paddling the canoe down the widening stream.

His mind raced, cursing fate and the circumstances of Kate's accident. If anything happens to her, he said over and over to himself, I'll make Marsha and Craig pay! He searched the banks for any sign any indication of other people.

Still he paddled on; Kate grew restless as the fever from her arm spread throughout her body. She tossed her head from side to side, only stopping when Morgan tore his shirt into strips, dipping each in the cool stream and laid the cool compresses across her forehead, his quiet voice breaking through her sleep.

The poison spread; Kate's restless movements were interspersed with her murmurs. Morgan bent low to hear her, "What is it Kate?" He again tucked the blanket around her in an attempt to quiet her thrashing.

Kate opened her eyes wide, yet not seeing Morgan at all, the fever had sent Kate back to a time in the orphanage as she whispered silent pleas to her unseen guardian, "I'll be good ... I promise... why don't they like me? ...what's wrong with me, sister? I can do it myself... I don't need anybody. I can do anything...don't make me go through that again... just want somebody to love me ... why can't they love ...I'll be good ... don't leave me alone again ..."

"Hush, Kate," Morgan said his voice a soothing sound to Kate's ears. "You'll be okay," Morgan's face was tortured as he understood the silent prayer of his little waif. The curl of smoke on the horizon caught his eye and he raised an anguished face to follow its trail. Renewed hope gave Morgan the extra strength to send their canoe on the last leg of their journey. Morgan saw the dock and as he approached began shouting to attract as much attention as possible. A head appeared behind the cabin and then another from the cabin door. As Morgan pulled the canoe onto the shore the young couple walked cautiously down to the newcomer.

Morgan bent down and very gently picked up Kate cradling her against his chest, "She's been bitten by a water moccasin. Get me to the nearest hospital ... "Nobody said anything for a moment, and then the silent couple went into action. The young man ran to get his jeep and the woman going towards Morgan to touch Kate's arm.

Kate's eyes opened, she looked at the woman and then upwards to Morgan's face, her forehead creased as she tried hard to remember what had seemed so important, "Morgan," Her voice was little more than a whisper.

"Yes, love ..." Morgan held her tightly within his arms. "Don't talk, save your strength."

She moistened her dry lips," The canoe ... the beginners..." her eyes beseeched Morgan's to understand.

"We'll send help back, little one." Morgan said his eyes tender, worried on her flushed face. "I promise."

Kate's eyes closed again satisfied that everything would be okay. Morgan had promised.

Morgan's eyes never left Kate's face, but he spoke to the woman next to him. "We found the canoe this morning, washed downstream with the storm last night. We used it because we could get help sooner, can you contact the park ranger to look for them?"

"We've a radio inside," the woman said and hurried back to the cabin. The young man brought the jeep up and Morgan climbed in, carefully holding Kate.

CHAPTER 15

Morgan paced outside the emergency room of the small country hospital, his hand going through his already tousled hair. He looked up as the young man with the jeep came through the door. Morgan extended his hand towards him, "I don't think I've told you thanks, I don't know what I'd have done ..." he paused, his eyes straying back to the emergency doors. Looking back at him, Morgan smiled, "The name's Morgan Buchanan. If there's ever anyway I can return the favor, just ask."

"Jeff Martin," the young man returned, "and no thanks are necessary, we're just glad we could help."

"All the same," Morgan said firmly his assurance coming through, "Thanks." Silence fell between the two as Morgan again watched for the doors to open.

"Should ... do you or your wife have any family that you should contact ...?" Jeff asked.

"I've already called one of her brothers," Morgan answered, "He'll contact the rest." He turned towards the room where Kate laid, "Damnit! What's taking them so long?!"

"I'm sure they're doing everything they can to help her," Jeff offered, aware of Morgan's frustration at not being able to do anything to help. "You're tired, why not sit down," He paused, "try and get some rest, there's nothing you can do ..." his voice trailed away.

"I'm not leaving until they tell me she's going to be alright," His voice was determined, he turned set eyes on Jeff, "I appreciate your concern," Morgan began, "but I'm not moving." He looked back at the doors, "You go on home, and ... thanks again."

Jeff nodded and reluctantly left; Morgan's powerful presence still felt. Morgan resumed his pacing his long strides making the hallway seem very small and confining. Don't give up, Kate, Morgan willed silently to the small body in the other room. Don't leave me, you've so much to live for ... his mind refused to dwell on any possibility other than her recovery.

Finally, her doctor emerged, he looked with added concern at the distraught Morgan. "How's Kate?" Morgan's voice rasped out.

"Not good," Dr. Kraco told him, "We've given her the serum but ... so much time has elapsed between when she was bitten and when we were able to inject her," He paused watching Morgan's dark complexion pale, "She's small but she's in excellent physical health and" he touched Morgan's shoulder, "she's a fighter."

Morgan nodded, "How long before she's home free, Doc?"

"We'll know within the next twenty-four hours; the poison can paralyze her lungs ... heart ... If it settles in any of her vital organs ..." He stopped to let his words take effect, "You had the tourniquet on," He noticed Morgan's torn shirt for the first time, "With the antivenin, there's a chance we'll be able to neutralize the poison and its effects. Right now, we just wait and monitor for any changes."

"Can I see her?" Morgan asked.

"If I told you no, would you sit down and wait until later?" the doctor asked shrewdly.

"No," Morgan said, standing to his full six-foot height, "I'm afraid I wouldn't."

"I didn't think so," Dr. Kraco said, "I'll arrange for you to go in, more to keep from having two patients rather than the one I've got."

"Thanks, Doc," Morgan said, and pushed the door open. The white walls of the emergency room seemed to echo its starkness. His focus was on the shine of red hair under the bright lights. The oxygen mask covering her face made her look very small on the hospital bed. Morgan was very careful not to touch the tubes going into her arm as he bent to kiss her forehead, his hands going gently to push her hair away from her face. The presence of the doctor and two nurses didn't seem to matter, as Morgan pulled up a chair beside her bed, out of their way but close enough to touch Kate's hand. Only then did he look up at the doctor. He dared the doctor with his eyes to tell him to leave or even move.

"Sir..." the nurse began.

"Let him stay," the doctor said, he watched as Morgan tenderly held Kate's hand between his own large ones. "She can use all the help he can give her." Morgan's silent nod spoke his thanks to the doctor, and he turned back to Kate.

In sleep, her lashes lay dark against her skin, the quick rise and fall of her rapid breath, told Morgan she was fighting for her life. He gently squeezed her hand, "I'm here, Kate, don't give up, you can do it" He murmured, "I'm not leaving you, I'm right here." His fingers moved soothingly over her hand, still holding on to her.

The day dragged on, hour after hour, Morgan dozed only to awake at the slightest movement or sound from Kate. Patrick and Leigh arrived late in the afternoon, their concern for Kate hiding their surprise at the sight of Morgan as well. His usually dark complexion pale, lines seemed permanently etched across his face, his entire body tensed for battle. Only his hands were different, they had not moved for they still cupped Kate's fingers in his own. It was almost as if he were giving his strength to Kate through the touch of his hands on hers. He nodded at Pat and Leigh, a slight smile to welcome them.

"How's she doing?" Leigh whispered, one hand touching Morgan's shoulder the other held tight by Pat.

"She's holding her own ..."Morgan said, his voice croaked," ... barely... "His voice broke, "she's so small and she's been fighting for so long." His despair wrung Leigh's heart and told her more than any words could have done.

Pat's voice broke into the silence, "What were you doing in the middle of the forest? I thought you were going to Mike's cottage?"

Morgan sighed, "Well, the cottage wasn't a cottage, those rumors we heard about the mansion in the hills were true. Kate fought with Craig, "his name was said through clenched teeth, "and I fought with Marsha, they retaliated by taking us on a picnic lunch," he paused remembering, "And leaving us two hundred miles in the middle of the forest alone." He waited seeing Kate spear fishing, and swimming in the creek seemed to have happened more than just a few days away." They hadn't reckoned on Kate's knowledge of the woods, we slept in a lean-to and feasted on trout," He smiled and reached to touch her cheek, "A storm last night washed a canoe our way, we were coming home. I splashed her, she reached into the water to even the score," His voice shook, "... a water moccasin happened to be passing by. I paddled to the nearest home and they brought us here." Silence filled the room until Morgan spoke again, full of grim determination, "I blame myself for letting anything happen to Kate, I promised to take care of her ..."

"Morgan it wasn't your fault ..." Pat began only to be silenced by Morgan.

"If anything happens to her, I'll ruin Moreland Int. and Warner!" He looked up to meet Pat's eyes, the cold, frozen hatred communicating to him, Morgan meant every word.

The nurse arrived then, checking Kate's vital signs and adjusting the tubes flowing to her arms. She then turned to Kate's visitors, "I'm afraid you'll have to leave, there's a waiting room in the hallway we'll keep you posted."

Pat and Leigh walked to the door, turning to wait for Morgan. "All of you," the nurse said firmly, looking at Morgan's dark head.

"I'm not going anywhere," Morgan said his voice low but authoritative, "I'm staying right here, Kate needs me ..."

"Sir..." the nurse began used to dealing with difficult situations, "she's asleep and not aware of anything or anyone in this room."

"She knows ..." Leigh said meeting Morgan's anguished glance. "We'll wait outside, Morgan, we're here if you need us," and she and Pat slipped from the room.

"Her doctor said I could stay" Morgan said finally to the nurse, "and I'm staying..."

The nurse stood silent for a moment and then followed in the wake of Pat and Leigh.

"It's back to being just you and me, Kate," Morgan whispered, his eyes caressing each feature on her face, "...together we'll win, Kate. You're such an independent little thing. "He talked more to himself than for Kate to hear, "You've managed for yourself for so long, you can get along without needing anybody. But Kate," He paused, "You need me, like I need you; I never thought I'd need another person like I do you." He smiled faintly, again raising a hand to touch her face, "Even in my wildest dreams did I picture a red haired elf taking over my life, now you are my dream ... " Morgan bent his head, "Don't leave me, Kate," he finished, searching her face, willing her to get better.

Almost featherlike Morgan felt Kate's fingers move, held between his own she tried to squeeze his hand. Tears flowed unheeded down Morgan's face, "We're going to make it," Morgan smiled, relieved. He knew that Kate knew he was there, and that was all that mattered. He'd tell her how he felt later. He turned to get comfortable in the chair, his head resting on the back, his hand still holding Kate's, Morgan finally slept.

A gentle shake of his shoulder and Morgan sat upright, his first glance at Kate. Watching her gentle breathing, Morgan turned to see who was there. A smile covered tired lines on his face, "Hello, Danny."

"How's she doing?" Danny asked.

"Better," Morgan answered wearily, "But she's not out of the woods yet."

"How are you?" Dan asked, taking in his exhaustion.

"Don't worry about me," Morgan said, "As soon as they tell me Kate's going to be all right ... so will I."

"...Two for the price of one?" Dan smiled watching Morgan.

"Something like that," Morgan agreed reaching out to touch Kate's face.

As his fingers left her cheek, Kate opened her eyes and saw Morgan and Danny, licking dry lips, she whispered, "You look terrible Morgan! Are you all right?"

"ME?" Morgan squeezed her hand, "I'm terrific...now," He added smiling at the sleepy figure, "how do you feel?"

"Dopey... "Kate murmured.

"Well, I can see you're back to normal," Dan interjected bending to kiss Kate's cheek, "I've always said you were a bit on the Dopey side."

"You would," Kate said, "What are you doing here by the way?" She creased her forehead in concentration.

"The whole crew is just outside the door," Dan continued, "You gave us quite a scare ..." He looked up at Morgan, "He was so worried he wouldn't leave ..."

"Morgan...?" Kate questioned carefully watching his face, only then realizing he was still holding her hand.

"Don't listen to Dan, "Morgan said and sent a withering look at his friend, "I just wanted to know you were going to be fine."

Kate grinned, "I seem to remember you telling me I would be ... I thought that settled the matter ..."

"It wasn't quite that simple, little one," Morgan chuckled, "Like always, you had to worry us a while."

Dan walked to the door, "I'll let the others know you're back to normal." and he left whistling.

"Thanks," Kate murmured unsure of how to interpret Morgan's look and concern.

"For what?"

"For caring," Kate said watching his dark eyes that seemed to melt her.

"Oh Red," Morgan said softly, "If you only knew how much I care," his lips descended swiftly upon hers. Too soon he raised his head, "I'll be back...soon," he paused huskily, "See your family and then rest ... promise?"

Kate nodded her head, as the door opened, and her tribe of brothers entered quietly. Kate grinned, "Hey you guys, this isn't a morgue ... I'm fine, see?"

As they filled the room, Morgan walked to the door and raised a warning finger at the group, "Don't tire her out," and he was gone.

"Hey Kate..." Mike whistled, "That's some guardian angel!"

" .. He had these doctors and nurses jumping. "

" .. He wouldn't leave you, stayed the entire night ..."

"You sure had us worried!" Leigh finished as they all spoke at once.

"I know ..." Kate said, biting her lower lip, "it's so good to have you all here."

After ten minutes, Kate's eyelids started to droop, and Mike ushered all of the Ryan clan out the door. "You heard the boss," he teased, "Get some rest, sis," he added. "We'll be back later, if Morgan will let us in!"

Kate blushed, her eyes closing sleep and contentment washing over her tired body. Waking later, she was surprised to find Morgan back at her side. "I thought you went to get some sleep?" Kate asked, thinking how nice it was to wake and see him.

"I did," Morgan assured her, his body rising from the chair to tower over her, "I just wanted to be sure I wasn't dreaming ... you really are better."

"Fit as a fiddle ..." Kate assured him, shifting her weight to sit up, wincing at the ache that flowed throughout her body, "If I got bit on the arm ... "Kate asked, "how come my whole-body hurts?"

"Reaction to the poison ... you fought quite a battle you know," Morgan answered solemnly.

"I ... don't think I fought it alone ..." Kate murmured, "I had the feeling you were there, too."

"I was," Morgan said shuddering at the memory of what might have been.

"It's been quite a vacation, hasn't it?"

"Vacation!?"

"... To the cottage," Kate added, "the hike, canoe trip... "She grinned mischievously, "Like I once told you ... you certainly show a girl an exciting time!!"

"Minx!" Morgan laughed, "It's not quite what I had planned but I'm glad to know you weren't ... bored!"

"There wasn't time!" Kate smiled, "Have you talked with Mike, Marsha's father?"

"No." Morgan said, "Nor do I intend to ..."

Kate raised a questioning eyebrow, Morgan continued, "I think it's best that it's to be quite some time before I see any of them, I'll not be accountable for my actions ..." His jaw tensed, "Because of their machinations you could have died!" a tiny muscle in his jaw jerked, "We'll do business elsewhere ... "

"Can you afford that?" Kate asked concerned.

"That and a lot more," Morgan assured her, "Do you feel up to talking for a while?"

"Changing the subject again?" Kate asked.

"Yes!" Morgan said meeting Kate's eyes, he reached for her hands, and sat beside her on the bed. "Kate ..." he paused as if searching for the right words, "Kate ..."

"I don't bite," Kate replied hoping to make things easier for him. "I know what you're going to say anyway ..."

"You do?"

"Sure, now that your connections with Moreland are over, we no longer have a reason to pretend we're engaged." She twisted the emerald flower on her hand, she swallowed hard and held out the ring to him, "Thank you, Morgan, it's been a very... enjoyable... experience."

Morgan stared at the ring in Kate's hand; his hand covered hers, the ring hidden between them both. "No Kate!" Morgan said, at last. "You're right I do want to end our mock engagement, because little one," He touched her cheek ... I'd like to make it a real one ..."

Kate's eyes flew open and she stared at Morgan in puzzlement, "But...why...?"

"Why, Kate?" Morgan began searching for words, "Because I love you ... because the thought of losing you is more than I could bear ..." He bent and kissed her nose, her eyes, and finally her upturned lips. Kate's arms circled his neck, tears fell down her cheeks. At the taste of salt, Morgan raised his head, "Kate? I didn't mean to hurt you," He murmured.

"These ... these are tears of joy," Kate beamed, "Oh, Morgan, I love you so much ... the thought of walking out of your life..."

He kissed her again, "Does this mean you'll marry me?" Morgan asked holding her close.

"If you're sure you really want me?" Kate said.

"Let there be no doubt in your mind, my love ... I've wanted you since the first time I saw you ..." He reached out to curl his fingers in her hair, and pull her gently to him, "and it's gotten worse every day since ..." He again kissed her,

"Holding you in my arms when we were camping was my own private heaven and hell ... so close and yet I couldn't scare you or take advantage of your trust ... I came so close, Kate, to telling you how I felt then ..."

"I wish you had Morgan," Kate ran a finger over his lips, "We wouldn't have had to come back so soon ..." Lost in themselves, they didn't hear the door open.

"How touching..." Marsha's voice was like a whip across the room.

CHAPTER 16

"Get out!" Morgan said through clenched teeth, "the only thing keeping me from throwing you out is an old adage of never hurting a woman ... and I'm forgetting it very quickly. You could have killed her!" His words filled with contempt.

"Yes ... well ... that wasn't my idea," Marsha said quickly, "and we did go back, the very next day in fact, but you had already left."

Morgan stood up and took a step toward Marsha, she put up a hand to touch his arm, and "I need to talk to you, Morgan, privately... "She looked across at Kate, "I've something to tell you about ... "

"I don't really care what you have to say!" Morgan responded forcibly guiding Marsha through the door. They almost collided with the nurse coming to announce the close of visiting hours.

Morgan turned back to Kate, only to have her smile and blow him a kiss, "I'll see you in the morning," Morgan said, his look tender and full of love.

"I'll be waiting," Kate told him, as he closed the door reluctantly.

Kate leaned dreamily back against the pillows; not even Marsha's outburst could dim her happiness. Morgan loves me! Kate hummed to herself; she slipped her ring back on her finger. She spoke to the nurse, who was busy checking her pulse and blood pressure, "How much longer before I can leave this place?"

"A couple more days, I'm sure," she responded, "Maybe less if your young man has his way."

Kate's golden laugh filled the room; my young man ... Morgan was really mine. She turned on the television to pass the time, mindlessly watching the proverbial detective show, her thoughts still on Morgan. The ringing of the telephone made Kate jump, she reached for it, hoping it might be Morgan.

"Hello," Kate answered.

"It's over," the woman said over the phone.

"I beg your pardon ..." Kate asked.

"You and Morgan," the caller laughed. "I told him... you know about the other men ..." A cold shudder went over Kate's body. "What other men?"

"Someone called Max ... and another one called Ryan O'Hara ... living with one, seeing another." Again, the laugh, "he won't be back, Kate O'Hara. He doesn't mix with married women, you know. That and he doesn't like lies and you're full of contradictions." This time the voice was little more than a sneer. "Your little Miss Perfect act didn't work. I suggest you get out of his life before he throws you out."

The click at the other end of the line, told Kate the caller... Marsha ... was done. Kate cradled the phone in her hands. Her dreams seemed shattered. The men! Kate laughed and then cried. I'm innocent! And yet it sounds so condemning. Morgan won't believe her ... he'll come to me and I'll explain. But will he believe me, a tiny voice asked? Love is built on faith and trusts ... Does Morgan have that trust? Do I have that faith in Morgan to believe in me?

Sadly, Kate shook her head. She threw her legs over the side of the bed and reached for the pencil the nurse had used on her chart.

Numbly, Kate rang for the nurse's aide. "May I have some paper, please ..." Kate asked, "and could I see my doctor right away?"

As she scurried away, Kate dialed the hotel her family was using. Minutes later Kate asked for Danny. "Hello, Danny?" Kate began, "I need ... to see you...no...No I'm fine...really... I just need to see you. I know its past visiting hours ... but I know you, Dan...You'll find a way..."She paused, "You always do ..." Kate hung up. With trembling hands, she began to write, Dear Morgan...

A week later, Ryan O'Hara's Exhibit opened in St. Louis. Critics raved at the natural almost human animals captured on film. The black and white contrast of the elderly couple silhouetted against the evening's sky. The child's intense concentration at the tiny caterpillar only inches away. These pictures talked, with a flick of a shutter, Ryan spoke.

Morgan wandered among the pictures, watching for just the slightest glimpse of a red thatch of hair. Despite himself, he was moved by the artistic delivery of the photographs. He wearily threaded his fingers through his hair, she has to be someplace, ever since he had received her note hoping that he would find happiness, but she had changed her mind, and she had left, disappeared. Her family was astonished, all but Danny, and he seemed to be missing, too.

It was then he saw a russet head. Too tall for Kate, Morgan reasoned walking quickly, but maybe Danny...

His hand on Dan's arm was firm, "Where is she?" Morgan asked his body tense as he waited for his answer.

"Hello, Morgan," Dan said. "I thought you might be here." He took a few steps toward the next picture, ignoring the warning signs of Morgan's temper.

Morgan let go of Dan's arm, his jaw tense as he followed behind Dan.

"Patience has never been very big with me ..." Morgan said cautioning Dan. "I've spent the last week going out of my mind looking for Kate. I know you helped her leave the hospital and I know you know where she's at."

"Why do you want to find her?" Dan asked studying Morgan's expression.

"Because, I love her, Damnit!" He said harshly as several people turned to stare, "and I don't think I can live without her ..." His voice spoke of his raw emotions--Danny gave a half smile.

"What about the other men?" again he waited for Morgan's reaction.

"Why I'm explaining this to you instead of Kate ..." Morgan ground out.

"Unless you convince me," Dan said flatly, "You'll never find Kate. I'll see to it..." He promised.

Morgan's anger left at the thought of never seeing Kate again, he looked searchingly at Dan's earnest serious face and knew he was the key to finding her. A reluctant nod and Morgan spoke, "I heard about the men. Marsha made sure of that ... I believe there are other men in Kate's life ..."

Dan turned away, only to stop as Morgan held his arm, "But not in the sense she meant." Morgan looked into Dan's anger, "I know Kate and I know that there's an explanation for them ..."

"And if there's not?" Dan reasoned.

"Then I don't care," Morgan exploded, oblivious to the stares of others, "Nothing she's done can change my feelings about her ... a dozen Max's ... Ryan's ... I'll still love her. Whether you help me or not I'll find her and until Kate tells me face to face, she doesn't love me ... I'll not leave her alone."

Dan stared at the flashing eyes and Morgan's clenched fists at his side. For what seemed an eternity, neither spoke. Finally, Dan raised his hand to clasp Morgan's, "I'll take you to Kate," he said slowly, "but first there's a few people you need to meet ..."

He led Morgan up to a rather grizzled white-haired man, who had a half-smoked cigar between his teeth. With one shrewd look, his eyes seemed to bore through to Morgan's very soul. "Morgan ..." Dan began, "I'd like you to meet Max ... Max Donovan."

Morgan's eyes flashed in sudden interest, he held out his hand, "Mr. Donovan ..." he said politely.

"Max," Dan added, "This is Morgan Buchanan..."

"I know who he is," Max said gruffly, he nodded towards a silhouette on the wall behind him. Morgan was startled, a puzzled frown crossing his forehead. The photograph was of a man, himself, his profile against the city of St. Louis. His features were only hinted at but the sheer strength and dominance of his personality against the rise of the buildings, the arch spoke volumes. The double exposure had captured both the city and the man.

Morgan turned back to Max and Dan. He pushed his hand through his hair, "Mr. Donovan there's a lot I don't understand ... fine ... tell me later. Right now, I just want to find Kate."

"And what happens when you find her?" Max asked.

"I'm hoping she'll marry me," Morgan said quietly, "I just can't imagine my life without her..."

Max reached out and touched his shoulder, "Welcome to the family, Morgan," he said, "Neither can we."

Kate leaned against the tree, her thoughts on Morgan. Idly she cast her pole into the water, the momentary splash of water disappearing down the stream. Birds circled overhead, and their cries echoed across the stream. Kate stared unseeing into the water; memories followed her even in her sanctuary. How long am I going to be haunted by his presence? She knew she had to pull herself together. Get on with her life, but oh Morgan. Kate cried; it seems so empty without you.

Leaving the hospital, convincing Dan and the doctor, Kate still felt the exhaustion. Her pole bobbed in the water, lost in thought, Kate was startled when the pole was taken from her hands.

"You're about to lose our dinner," Morgan said, his eyes seeming to devour her.

Kate's pleasure at seeing him turned to pain, "How did you know where I was?"

"Danny and a man by the name of Max Donovan ..." Morgan pulled in the fish and laid the pole against the tree. He sat down beside Kate, observing her too pale skin, the sad emerald eyes which seemed to fill her face. He noticed how thin she seemed, her flannel shirt and worn jeans hanging loosely about her. With a trembling hand, Morgan reached out and touched Kate's cheek. At his touch Kate flinched as if burned.

"Oh Morgan..." Kate cried, "Why did you come? How am I to ever forget you if you keep touching me?"

Her cry wrung Morgan's heart, "Oh Katie, my Katie ... I don't intend to let you forget me. I love you ... " He covered her mouth with his hand, "let me talk, love, please?" He took a deep breath, as much to steady his own trembling as Kate's, "I don't really understand why you left Kate, it doesn't really matter, you see," He paused to gently raise her hand to his lips, "only one thing does, you told me in the hospital, you loved me. I believed you then Kate just as I believe you still love me ... " He squeezed her hands, "There is nothing that can change how I feel for you, Kate ... I love you now as I'll love you tomorrow and next week ... next year. I can't imagine a life without you. But," He paused again, "if you tell me you made a mistake and don't love me ... I'll get out of your life for good."

"No, you don't love me!"

"Or no you can't deny you love me?" Morgan asked patiently.

"I can't tell you I don't love you," Kate said softly.

"Does that mean you are still a little bit in love with me?" Morgan asked solemnly.

"No," Kate smiled tremulously, "It means I love you hopelessly, unreasonable with my whole heart.

"Oh Kate," and Morgan crushed her to him, kissing her as a man drowning. Kate pressed herself closer to Morgan, her entire body coming alive under his touch, curling her fingers in his hair to bring his lips to hers again. Slowly and with great reluctance, Morgan held Kate beside him, looking into her eyes, "We have to talk, and Kate ... we need to bury your demons. I want to marry you, spend my life with you ... I want no shadows to mar our happiness. Why did you leave me? Telling me you had changed your mind?"

Kate rested her head against his chest, "I was afraid, when you heard about Max and Ryan, you'd be angry... I didn't want to see our love so new... so fragile destroyed. I thought my disappearance would be easier to accept. I couldn't stand to see you look at me like you look...at your mother."

"Oh, my love," Morgan kissed her again, his voice husky as he raised his head, "I knew you were innocent of anything even as Marsha spoke ... I told her so, told her it didn't matter if they were true. I would still love you."

"That must have been when she called me." Kate said marveling at the love she felt and saw from Morgan. "I never thought I would ever find somebody to love me despite my faults ... regardless of my past..."

"You underestimate your power, Red, I was lost from the first," He laughed, "I remember the first time I danced with you at the Country Club. You seemed to fit into my arms perfectly... I could feel you long after I sent you back to your table."

"But you were so angry with me!" Kate protested.

"You made things very hard on me ... I had a rough time concentrating with you so near and yet so far, and I thought you were engaged to Mike not Katrina. I couldn't understand how you could respond to me and marry someone else ..."

"Morgan," Kate interrupted, "about Ryan O'Hara ... "Morgan didn't want to let Kate talk, but she persisted," He's not really a person. When I first started out with Da ... people accepted me because of him. When he died, I needed help ... not because I couldn't do the work... but they didn't believe I could do it. A different name, an agent ... I could still do it. Max was an old friend of Da's ... he and I created Ryan O'Hara," Kate raised sparkling eyes to his, "I love you Morgan, I was afraid you wouldn't believe I could do the pictures."

"Kate," Morgan spoke sternly and then smiled to ease the seriousness of his tone, "I believe you can do anything you set out to do. I was very impressed by your pictures ... they tell me a great deal about you. Especially the double exposure ..."

"Max wasn't to use that one!" Kate cried.

"He did, and it was then I knew about Ryan and you, you didn't need to tell me, but I'm glad you did."

"No more shadows?" Kate smiled radiantly up at Morgan.

"No more shadows ... "he responded, pulling Kate to her feet and into his arms. "Now I think we'd better head back to your cabin? We've company."

"Here?" Kate was surprised.

"Max and Danny insisted on coming with me, I think we need to reassure them I haven't carried you off against your wishes!"

Linking her arm around Morgan's waist, his resting around her shoulder, they walked towards the small log cabin on the hill, "My wish," Kate said softly "is to live with you as your wife, your friend, your lover," Kate blushed, "and to fill your days with happiness."

187

"That's one wish, I can guarantee," Morgan said, tipping Kate's face up to meet his.

"Promise?" Kate said against his quickening breath.

"Promise," Morgan said and met her lips with a promise of his own.

EPILOGUE

Several years have passed, Morgan and Kate were married and the whole family, (minus his mother) was thrilled at how happy Kate was. Morgan was finally content. He was loved unconditionally, and Kate made him happy beyond all his expectations. R & B was growing by leaps and bounds; Kate still took her pictures and put on at least one exhibition a year. But this year she was severely hampered by being pregnant. Morgan wouldn't let her go off to her cabin or to set her camera up alone. He usually accompanied her, just to make sure that she was all right. He didn't want anything to mar Kate's happiness at the birth of their first child, or any other births from their children in the future.

Morgan was at work, and he was a lot easier to work for these days! He and Pat were considering enlarging their company when his intercom buzzed. "Morgan, here...Kate, what's wrong? Is it the baby? I'm on my way!"

Morgan grabbed his coat and was out the door leaving Pat to inform the rest of the clan about Kate. Kate insisted on Morgan having a driver until after the baby was born. She was sure that Morgan would drive like a madman coming home and taking her to the hospital, and she wanted to ensure that Morgan would be in one piece to be a father to their baby!

"Can't you go any faster? It seems like we're not moving at all! Kate's in labor, for God's sake!" Morgan kept up a running dialogue all the way home. When they reached the front door, he could see Kate at the window watching for them. "Keep the engine running, we'll be right back!" He was taking the front stairs two and three steps at a time. "Kate, are you, all right? How fast are the contractions coming?"

"Relax Morgan...we have plenty of time...Mary tells me that the first baby takes the longest to get here. The contractions are about six minutes apart." Kate was glowing and so excited to be having Morgan's baby. She couldn't wait to hold her own baby in her arms.

Within fifteen minutes they arrived at St. Luke's Hospital. Morgan filled out the insurance forms and they took Kate upstairs to the Maternity floor. He arrived shortly afterwards. Kate was hooked up to a fetal monitor and another one to her own vitals. She had changed out of her own clothes and was wearing a hospital gown. Morgan was shaking, he was so nervous. He didn't want to see Kate in pain; he didn't know how he would handle it. He worried all over again what kind of father he would be to their child. He already knew that Kate would be an exceptional mother, any child would be lucky to have her for a mother.

Kate's family started staggering in. The nurse let each one in to say 'Hello' and then shooed them out into the waiting room. The afternoon crept up on them and suddenly the contractions were coming one right after the other. Kate was examined by her Doctor and announced that she was fully dilated and ready for delivery. Kate was squeezing Morgan's hand so tightly; he didn't know if he would ever be able to use it again!

"Kate...give me one more big push...I can see the head crowning...in just a few minutes you'll be holding your own baby in your arms...that's right..." The rest was a blur as her baby was born.

Morgan couldn't take his eyes off the tiny red-haired bundle the doctor was holding. Their baby was finally here! "It's a little girl, Kate...and she looks just like her mother! She has red hair and everything, oh my God! She's beautiful!" Morgan told her with tears running down his face. Kate just smiled and then started pushing again with another contraction...

Her doctor quickly handed the baby over to the waiting nurse to be cleaned up. "Kate it looks like we're going to have another baby coming...we didn't hear two heartbeats...Even the sonogram didn't show two, but sure enough, here it comes..." Morgan was in shock. Two babies how could that be!

The second bundle of joy came into the world already crying. He didn't like the idea of his sister getting there before he did! He had a head of dark hair and did he have a good pair of lungs. Kate was crying she was so happy, two babies! Imagine a girl and a boy, what could be more perfect than that. Morgan leaned down to kiss Kate and whisper, "You just keep surprising me don't you Mrs. Buchanan?"

"Just keeping a promise, love...I promised to love you forever and to keep you guessing on a regular basis...I always keep my promises!" She smiled, "Whatever are we going to name them?"

"Good question, how about Fiona and Finnegan? Or Molly and Micah?" Morgan suggested so happy he didn't care what the babies were named.

"How do you feel about Riana for the little girl, and for her brother, Ronan?" Kate asked him.

"Riana Katherine Buchanan and Ronan Morgan Buchanan...I like it..." Morgan answered. "I love you, Kate...I can't tell you how much...it just doesn't seem enough. You've changed my life...you are looking at a very happy and content man. Thank you, love, for not giving up on me when I wouldn't let you be my secretary...you are the best thing to ever happen to me."

"Oh, Morgan..." Kate cried, "The best is yet to be...I promise!"

The End

Note from the Author

I want to personally thank you for your time and effort in the reading of this book. I love writing, and I owe it to my readers to do the best I can. The best source of input to influence my future efforts is your feedback. Please take just a few minutes to share whatever thoughts you may have on this book by going to https://www.amazon.com/author/m_dipaolo and submit a rating and, if you wish, some comments as well. I would really appreciate it.

ABOUT THE AUTHOR

Marcella (Marky) DiPaolo was raised as a farm girl in Moro, Illinois. She was one of six children, and they all interacted daily with their loving parents and grandparents who served as ideal role models for them as they grew up on the farm. Upon graduating from high school, Marcella started her career in business. She also went to college, initially to become an accountant. It was in the business world that she met the person with whom she wanted to share the rest of her life.

It didn't take long for the young couple to start filling up their home with children. It was in the raising of her own that she realized that working with kids was her passion. She decided that teaching was the direction she wanted to go. During the early years, she was the one that stayed home to watch the kids while her husband worked during the day and went to school at night to complete his education. Once finished, he spent his evenings with the children, so she could go on and complete her BA in Elementary Education and later getting a Masters with a concentration in mathematics.

After more than thirty-five years of teaching, she recently retired but continues to teach from time to time as a substitute at a local parochial school. Over the years, Mrs. D., as she is referred to by her students, was recognized for her teaching accomplishments having received several awards and other forms of recognition. 'Mrs. D' has certainly had a very special effect on a lot of young people, all of whom she still considers members of her 'extended' family.

Marcella has a lot of other interests as well. In addition to a voracious appetite for romantic plots and characters, she is also fond of adventure stories and mysteries. She also loves to watch sports, play golf, eat chocolate, and spend as much time as possible with her family.

Marcella's love of reading began at a very early age. However, she never dreamed she might become a writer until much later in life. Being somewhat addicted to historical romances, both in books and on the screen, she has been exposed to a lot of writing styles. This experience and her time on the farm, raising a family, and all those years in the classroom have provided her with a wealth of ideas to apply to her writing career.

Other Books Written by Marcella DiPaolo

Clear Water Bride Series
   Bargain Bride
   Troubled Bride
   Forgotten Bride
   Reluctant Bride
   Runaway Bride
Morgan Brothers Storm Series
   Above the Storm
   After the Storm
   Beyond the Storm
Pine City Chance Series
   Taking a Chance
   A Second Chance

www.ingramcontent.com/pod-product-compliance
Lightning Source LLC
Chambersburg PA
CBHW032134170626
46808CB00006B/2227